TOMAS

TOMAS

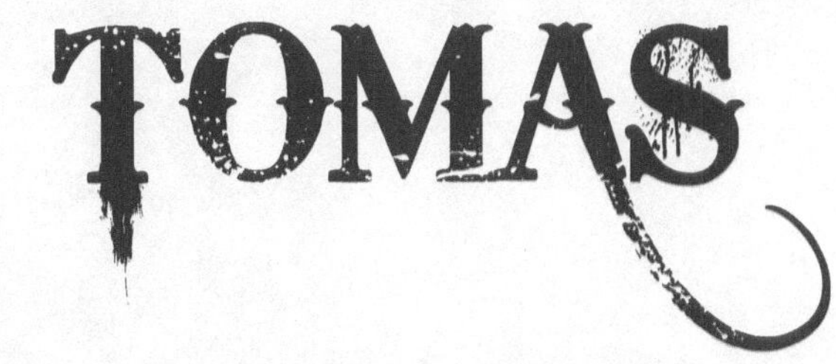

Porn Star Brothers Book 3

L.J. DIVA

★ Royal Star Publishing ★

Chances is an imprint of Royal Star Publishing
www.royalstarpublishing.com.au

This Collector's Edition paperback published in 2018
All Rights Reserved, Copyright ©L.J. Diva 2018

Trade Paperback ISBN: 978-1-925683-46-2
Case Laminate Hardcover ISBN: 978-1-922307-29-3
E-Book ISBN: 978-1-925683-45-5
A catalogue record for this book is available from the National
Library of Australia.

Cover design: Royal Star Publishing and Odyssey Books
Cover photos: CURAphotography/Shutterstock.com
Typesetting in Minion Pro by Royal Star Publishing

Dedications

In 2014 a vague idea to write a book about a porn star came to me. In 2015 the idea brewed and grew and when my idol, Jackie Collins, passed away, the idea flourished with a vengeance. Jackie Collins is the only inspiration in my life when it comes to writing. She had the passion, the brains, the ballsy rollicking attitude, and the kind of life that made me want to be her. Without her, these books would not exist, for I would not have had the inspiration to follow in the same 'write whatever you want' league. Without her, I will continue trying to write the kind of books she wrote. Real, ballsy, and bonkbustingly good.

Jackie, the Porn Star Brothers book series is dedicated to you as so many of my other books are. I thank you for the inspiration you have given me and hope you continue giving me, to go on and write more. I hope that you are well and having a good laugh wherever you are. I miss you and will continue doing so. Sometimes I think I feel you egging me on with my writing. Maybe that's true, and maybe it's just my rampant imagination; the same imagination that has given me the books I have written so far in my life. And sometimes, I really wished I could be you. You will forever be my idol and inspiration and I thank you. RIP, Miss Jackie C.

And to the three Stefanovic brothers, Carlos, Pedro, and Tomas, without whom I would not have had names for my porn stars.

TOMAS

July 1977

The pounding on the door woke Tomas Stephanopoulos from a deep slumber. He heard his father stumble through the house to answer it, only to hear a man burst in demanding to know where Pedro was.

Sliding out of bed, he pulled a t-shirt on and went into the lounge room. "What's going on?" He eyed the big brute of a man standing in their home.

Spiros sighed. "Can you see if Pedro is in his room, Tomas?"

After examining his father's expression for a moment, he turned and walked into Pedro's room. Empty. He went back to his father. "Not here." His eyes moved to their large windmill-shaped wall clock. "But then it's probably too early for him to be here. Why are you looking?"

The man, Magnus, was guarded. "He left a gig early. Mr Poulos wondered if he'd come back here and was okay."

"You couldn't have called?" Tomas asked, intrigued

by what was happening.

Magnus nodded. "Forgive my intrusion." He backed out the door, and Spiros shut, locked, and bolted it behind him.

"That was strange." Tomas crossed his arms. "Very strange."

"Not really." Jenny emerged from the bedroom. "Especially since…" Her hand flew to her mouth and she sobbed.

Tomas saw the letter in her hand and took it when she held it out. "Dear Mama and Papa, something bad has happened and I must leave. I'm okay and will call when I can. I love you both, Pedro."

"What?" Spiros thundered. "Another son has left us. What is it with these two boys? The eldest and the youngest have both gotten themselves into trouble and left instead of staying and sorting it out. What did I raise? Criminals? They should be ashamed of themselves." He slumped onto the couch. "They should be ashamed."

Tomas looked from his father to his mother, who sat beside her husband, to the letter. It wasn't possible. Just not possible. First Carlos, then Pedro. What the hell was happening for his brothers to be leaving so suddenly? Why hadn't they heard him come home? Why hadn't he woken them and said something? He wondered what the man at the door was telling his boss. That Pedro wasn't there? Why had he left work early? He never leaves early. Wasn't it a birthday party for the boss's daughter? So what happened for Pedro to take off before the job was done? He re-read the note. Something bad has happened. What could that be? What could it mean? With both Carlos and Pedro in trouble, it was time someone found out.

*****

Tomas went to work later that morning at the Mykonos Desert Resort, the same resort Carlos had worked. He was the personal trainer in the hotel gym and started at nine every morning, much to the women's delight, as many were also clients of Carlos.

"Oh, my dear." Bette Olander held out her bejewelled seventy-year-old hands to him. "I have heard the terrible news that your other brother has left."

Jesus, news travelled fast on the Greek grapevine.

"How did you hear that, my dear Bette?" Tomas took her hands and air-kissed both cheeks. "*We* only just found out early this morning."

"Well…" She glanced around to see if anyone else was watching. "I heard it from Bertha, who heard it from Willow, who swears she overheard two police officers talking about a seaplane that had disappeared without booking a flight plan, and that the DJ from Santorini had disappeared with the boss's daughter. Well…" She stepped closer to him. "I remember you telling me about your brothers and what they do, and I put two and two together. Especially since Carlos had already gone. I'm so sorry."

Tomas breathed in. "So am I. Now, do you want your workout session?"

She looked surprised. "You don't want to talk about it?"

Shaking his head, he said, "Not today, Bette. Let's get you onto the bike." He guided her over to the exercise bike and started her off. "Five minutes and then we move on. Gotta get you warmed up."

She mounted the bike in her deluxe velvet workout tracksuit, with the bejewelled collar to match her bejewelled hands, ears and wrists. Bette Olander never did anything half-assed. Why would she when she had millions to her name and clothed herself in the best those millions could buy? Jewels adorned her at all times. Her feet were swathed in jewelled kitten heels, and anything she wore had some sort of shiny, sparkly ornament on it.

At seventy, she'd had her share of rich husbands who provided her with rich homes and anything else their money could buy. Now, in her twilight years, she was spending it how she liked, when she liked, and on whom she liked, and she liked Tomas Stephanopoulos very much.

Although, she thought he leant more to the male side of things, she wasn't in it for sex. She'd given up on *that* back in her fifties. No, she liked Tomas because he made her feel special, wanted, and like a young girl again. Besides, she'd already had one closeted gay husband and wasn't after another one. No, Tomas was simply a young man who made her feel alive. And she recommended him to all of her friends, telling all of those rich snobby Miami women who either had no husbands or no sex lives with their husbands to come down to Mykonos and spend the summer with Tomas. He would get them into the best shape of their lives.

She studied him as she cycled. Five eleven-ish, jet-black hair, dark brown eyes, in the best condition a man could be in. Abs that you could eat food off, arms that could carry you, and legs that could wrap around you. Yes, he was a fine specimen of a man, regardless of which way he turned.

Bertha finally made it through the door dressed from top to bottom in white spandex that showed off the figure she'd worked so hard for. "So sorry I'm late, dear Tomas, I was having a massage from that new man they've hired to replace your brother. He's okay, but not as good looking." At fifty-nine, Bertha St John was twice widowed and twice engaged. This time it was to a twenty-five-year-old stud she'd picked up in Miami the year before. With the plastic surgery she'd had to look younger, she looked forty, and he'd been the trainer she'd gone to when she wanted to lose weight and tighten up. And she tightened up all right. He tightened her up in ways she'd never known and promptly suggested they get married. Now she was waiting until her sixtieth to do so.

"That's okay, Bertha." Tomas air kissed her. "You can warm up on the bike. Bette, time to change." He escorted Bette to the stretching machine, and Bertha took her place.

"How are you, dear, with your brother being gone?" Bertha asked, patting her dyed brown bun into place.

Tomas sighed. It had been this way when Carlos had left, and now they were reliving it with Pedro. "We're fine. Obviously, they thought it was time for them to leave for bigger pastures than the Greek

Islands. They have their things." He shrugged. "Whatever they need to do, they're doing it."

"I'm finally here." Willow Bertran floated through the door. "Oh, Tomas." She came over to him. "I am *so* sorry about your brother. The police are involved, and now that nightclub owner wants to press charges against poor Pedro." Her blue-green bejewelled kaftan settled around her. "I'm so sorry."

Tomas frowned. "What do you mean, the police are involved? What charges?"

"Oh, my dear." She took his hand. "Do you not know?" She looked over at Bette and Bertha. "Have none of you heard?" They shook their heads and stopped exercising. "Well…" Willow settled in for a long chat. "It seems that Pedro was DJing at the going away party Andros Poulos was having for his daughter, Angelina. She's going to Juilliard in New York, you know." She fluttered her lashes. "Oh, I love New York, it's so lovely, especially in the fall."

"Get on with it, Willow," Bertha told her.

"Oh." Willow fluttered. "Well, it seems that sometime during the party Pedro and Angelina were caught in the alley and Poulos demanded they stop, but Pedro hit him over the head and then hit the bodyguard over the head, and they have both left the island for the mainland." She gasped for breath.

"They're in Athens?" Tomas muttered, thinking about the new information.

"Doesn't mean they're *still* in Athens," Willow said. "But at least you know they're not here anymore."

Tomas sighed; a deep guttural sigh that filled him

as he breathed in and then left him on the exhale. "At least we know something. But what are the charges?"

"Assault on Poulos and the bodyguard, rape and kidnap," Willow said.

Tomas's frown deepened. "Rape and kidnap? Who'd he rape and kidnap? The daughter? Angelina? How old is she anyway?"

Willow touched a finger to her lip. "Eighteen, I think."

"Well, that's hardly rape and he..." His voice trailed off as he remembered the red marks on his brother's back that morning in the bathroom. He'd asked if she was legal. Pedro had said he'd hoped so. Shit! "Do they know for a fact Pedro kidnapped her?"

"Well..." Willow's gaze wandered off so she was looking at the ceiling. "Not really."

"What do you mean, *not really*?" he asked.

"Well," she repeated. "They're taking Poulos's story as gospel."

"So, he could be lying to get my brother into trouble?" Tomas sighed once more and scratched his head. "What is it with my brothers getting into trouble? What is with these people wanting to blame my brothers..." He wandered over to the floor-to-ceiling windows and gazed out over the ocean. "What the hell is going on?"

"Tomas, darling," Willow called. "Are we getting on with our session?"

He heaved another sigh and turned around to see other guests had come in for their morning workout. "Of course, of course, let's get to work."

*****

Tomas hit up the resort's beach bar at lunchtime. "Hey, Antonio."

"Hey, man, haven't seen you for a while." Antonio was shaking a martini for a guest. "Here you go, ma'am." He slid it toward her then glanced at Tomas. "What can I get you?"

"A juice, and news on my family."

Antonio stopped what he was doing to stare at Tomas. "Yeah, I heard about Pedro. Disappeared like Carlos, huh?"

Tomas raised his brows and knocked back the drink Antonio gave him. "Seems so. What have you heard?"

Antonio threw a smile at a guest and took another order. "That he got into it with a club owner on Santorini, attacked him, and now there are charges."

Tomas sighed. He'd been doing a lot of that lately. "Yeah." He watched Antonio flirt with the girl. "That's what I heard. But what I don't get is this only happened in the early hours of this morning, yet everyone knows more than the family does. And besides which…" He stopped while Antonio served another customer. "How come the cops haven't knocked on our door yet?" He eyed off the good looking, lightly tanned, dark-haired guy a few paces away. They guy eyed him back and smiled. Tomas blanched and looked away.

"You don't know they haven't. They could be at your place right now."

Tomas thought about it. "Yeah. Jesus, I won't know

anything more until I get home."

Antonio handed a margarita to a customer. "Any news on Carlos?"

Tomas shook his head. "Nothing. We've been told the charges have been dropped, but no letter, no call, nothing." He glanced over at the hot stud that was still standing nearby. Teeny tiny red swim briefs held a huge package together. A soft gathering of chest hair spread across lean, tanned muscles and down into the briefs. He saw the man looking with a cocked brow and even cockier grin and reddened. "I gotta go. Let me know if you hear anything," he told Antonio and walked toward the hotel.

*****

When Tomas arrived home at five-thirty, he found his mother crying over the hot meal she was making. "Mama." He moved to her side and held her in his arms. "Mama."

"Oh, Tomas, what are we going to do?" she sobbed.

"About what? Tell me what's happened." He stroked her hair as he gently swivelled his body left to right in a semicircle, like rocking a baby to soothe and calm.

"The police," Jenny cried into his chest. "They were here today asking about Pedro. But I didn't tell them anything. What *could* I tell them? That my son had disappeared?" She sniffled.

"Did they hurt you?" He pulled back to look into his mother's eyes. "Did they touch you, or hurt you, or even," he looked around, "wreck the place looking for him?"

She shook her head. "No. They checked his room, looked in the others, asked me a bunch of questions. But no, they didn't touch me, or hit me."

"Who? Who didn't touch you, or hit you?" Spiros walked into the kitchen. "Who?"

"The police were here asking about Pedro," Tomas told him, seeing a mirror image of himself.

Spiros sighed and ran a hand through his thick black hair. "They were at the shop today too. Asked a bunch of questions. Stupid bloody cops." He saw his wife's tear-stained face and gently pulled her into his arms. "There, there, we'll get through this. I don't know how, but we will." He looked at Tomas. "Have *you* got any idea what your idiot brothers have done, or are up to?"

"Why would I?" Tomas shook his head. "But it seems the whole island has heard more than we have."

"How could they do this?" Spiros hissed. "To their mother. We did not raise them that way."

"This may not have anything to do with what they did," Tomas said. "*We know* they'd never hurt women, *we know* they'd never shoot anyone, or assault anyone. So maybe they were just in the wrong place at the wrong time."

"Rubbish," Spiros said. "My boys have gotten themselves into something *they* can get themselves out of."

*****

On Saturday, Tomas spent the weekend on Santorini to see if he could find out what was going on. He walked the island by day and went to SantorPoulos at night. Striding into the club, he saw a new DJ on stage, but the place was only half full. Most of the crowd was standing around drinking or talking. Making his way over to the bar he ordered a beer. "I thought this place was jumping? A friend of mine told me it was the place to be on Santorini."

Mikos, the bartender, grimaced. "It used to be, but the reason the tourists came here left."

"What do you mean?" Tomas frowned. "Was there food poisoning or something?"

Mikos laughed. "Nah, man. The DJ flipped his lid and assaulted the boss out back in the alley." He flicked his head in the direction. "Took off with the boss's daughter, apparently. No one knows where they've gone." He went to serve another customer.

Tomas looked around as he sipped his beer. The place was a tourist haven for skimpily clad women and hot men in shirts and shorts. The DJ was good, but not his brother.

"You want anything to eat?"

Tomas turned around to see Mikos. "No, thanks. This is fine for now." He lifted his beer slightly. "So, what's this new DJ like then?"

"He's all right." Mikos poured a beer. "Not as good looking as the last one, not as hot as the last one, and not as good on the decks as the last one."

"He was that good, huh." Tomas hid a grin.

"Yeah," Mikos said. "He was *that* good *and* better."

Tomas stayed for another beer. The club, and club scenes in general, were not his thing, but Pedro's, so the loud music was getting to him. Seeing no one he knew, he left and waited outside for a while, surprised to see Andros Poulos leaving by a side exit.

"I want Athens searched," he was saying as he buttoned up his blazer. "Clearly they were taken to the mainland, and clearly they were going for the long haul with the amount of luggage there was. In the meantime, I'm going to get a private investigator to check into flights out of the country to see if they took off overseas. I want you to get the information I want. Regardless of how you get it." He stepped into the back seat of his car.

"Yes, Mr Poulos." The burly bodyguard shut the door and walked around to the front, getting behind the wheel.

So, that's *Andros Poulos,* Thomas thought, trying to see through the dark night and club lights, but he couldn't get a good look. He wandered over to the exit to see the car heading straight down the road and up the hill. "How am I going to get any information about what's going on?" he muttered.

"Had enough already?"

Tomas spun around. "Huh?"

Mikos lit a cigarette. "Of the club? Had enough of the club already?"

Tomas gave a small laugh. "Yeah, clubs aren't really my sort of thing." He shrugged and tried to get more information. "My friend insisted I come to see the DJ, but he's not here so, not much point me staying. I think my friend will be disappointed that he's gone. She really talked him up and said how packed the place was."

"Yeah." Mikos took a long drag. "It was, but he bolted Thursday morning, and when everyone finds out he's not working, they leave."

"Thursday? You mean two days ago?" Tomas asked innocently.

"Yeah man," Mikos said. "Two freakin' days. He's gone for two freakin' days and the tourists are down by half. Mr Poulos ain't happy."

"No. I guess he wouldn't be," Tomas agreed. "This DJ must have been something for you to lose half your patronage in two days."

"Yeah," Mikos said, drawing back. "He was something. Pedro Stephanopoulos. Hot stud. Drew the women and men in every night he was here. The place was packed to the rafters, and more were lined up outside to get in, but never could because no one ever left the club until he left the stage. Ten hours he was on stage. The women loved him."

"Wow. Pity I missed him," Tomas said, leaning against a stone wall. In actual fact, he had seen Pedro the year before work a crowd for the same amount of time and marvelled at his stamina and extreme talent. He was proud of him for achieving his dreams of being a DJ and being in the music industry. He went in harder. "So, if he's taken off with the boss's daughter like all the rumours are saying, that must make things awkward."

Mikos shrugged nonchalantly. "The boss is like a

bear with a sore paw, yelling at everyone. Fired two kitchen staff yesterday, but his assistant had to hire two more just to keep the food going. Poulos doesn't care; he's got bigger things to worry about than his club."

"Must have cared about being assaulted by the guy that took off with his daughter? Was she underage; is that why he's pissed?"

Mikos flicked his cigarette to the ground where he stepped on it and shook his head. "She's eighteen, old enough to go off with a guy if she wanted. She was going to some big school overseas, so he had no problem with that."

"Was the assault bad?" Tomas asked. "He seemed okay when he left just now."

"Not too bad." Mikos opened the side door. "Took a trash can lid to the back of the head. So did the bodyguard. No one knew they were out there for about two hours. But not my business. You coming back in?" He held the door open.

Tomas put up a hand. "No, thanks. I think I'll get going. Let my friend know he's not here anymore."

"Suit yourself." Mikos let the door close on its own.

Well, that's interesting, Tomas thought. *But if Pedro did assault him, one, why did he do it, and two, why has he left the country?* He took the path back along the beach wondering what Andros was up to. *What in the hell is going on? Two brothers within weeks of each other and now I'm here on my own. What about me? What do I do now? What about mama? Did they care what she thought, or did they think our parents would be better off without them and their troubles sticking around? And papa? He was all but ready to give up and disinherit them. How could he? He raised us better than what he thinks they've done. It's as if he doesn't care if they've even done it. The cops on our doorstep are enough to make him believe they have, and that isn't fair.*

He reached his hotel and went up to his room. Opening the balcony doors, he stood staring at the distant lights of the islands and the way they mingled with the millions of stars in the sky that enveloped them *and him* with their sheer power. It was an awesome sight you couldn't get anywhere else.

He sighed. "Carlos, Pedro, where are you? Where the *hell* are you?"

*****

Sunday morning, Tomas walked around Santorini asking people about Andros and whether they knew anything about the assault on Thursday morning. No one did so he headed home, tired, dejected, and annoyed.

Maybe I should just let them go? Whatever has happened they're now off living their own lives. At least I hope they are... "Oh, sorry." He reached out to the person he'd bumped into. "Hey..."

"Hey..."

"I...sorry...I...did you drop anything." Tomas became flustered as he looked around.

"No, got everything," the man said and stepped out

of the way as passengers from the ferry jostled them aside.

Tomas moved with him. "I, uh, saw you the other day, didn't I?"

"At the beach bar." The man nodded.

Tomas felt the flutter; the weird, unusual flutter in his stomach. "Yeah." He stared at the six foot hunk before him. "Yeah."

The hunk smiled. "Do you work at the resort?"

"Yeah," Tomas said for the third time. "I'm the personal trainer in the gym."

"Oh." The man cocked an interested brow. "I've been wondering if I should get into the gym while on holiday."

"Are you staying at the resort?" Tomas took a step closer.

"I am." The man took a step closer.

"Maybe you should come in for a session."

"Maybe I should."

Tomas stared.

The man stared.

"I uh." Tomas took another step. "I'm back at work tomorrow."

"Do you do private sessions?" The man removed his sunglasses.

Tomas drowned in aqua blue eyes such as he'd never seen. Bluer and more aqua than the ocean surrounding them. He breathed in. "Um, yeah, I do, at night."

"I'll have to book you in then." He took a step closer and ended up toe to toe with Tomas.

Tomas swallowed, his throat clenched, his stomach clenched and it was freaking him out. "Please do," he finally managed.

*****

"Tomas, darling," Bette said Monday morning. "Have you thought of leaving the nest?" She was straddling the bike in the resort gym.

"Have never thought about it." He helped Bertha with her weight exercises.

"Now that Carlos and Pedro are gone, what will you do?" she continued.

Tomas moved on to Willow who was standing on the vibrating belt machine.

Willow was groaning in pleasure, hanging onto the machine head as if it was a man's as he pleasured her with his tongue. "Oh, God, this is good. Oh, God."

"Don't overdo it," Tomas told her before answering Bette. "I don't know what I'll do. Even though this is my home, so is Australia. Maybe I'll have to reconsider my options now."

"You're still young," Bertha added to the conversation. "You could travel and see the world before settling down with a young lady."

"Or an older one." Willow sighed as she stepped off the machine. "Oh, God that was so good."

"Or if you aren't interested in *those* things," Bette slyly said. "Someone *else* to settle down with."

Tomas flashed her a look. "And what do you mean by that?"

Bette, for all her years, didn't back down. "Tomas, darling, *we know.*"

"Know what?" He glanced around the gym to see who was watching or listening.

"That you are of the opposite persuasion," she said, getting off the bike and going to his side. "It's okay dear, that's what we love about you; that you're not interested in getting us into bed, or trying to charm us to get our money. You're the kind of young man every older woman wants in her life."

"And what would that be?" He stared down at her, his heart pounding in his chest. He'd never discussed his sexual orientation with anyone. He'd never needed to. He just wasn't interested in dating. The opposite sex or otherwise. He didn't feel sexual toward anyone, so had remained single. He was only twenty-two after all.

"Gay, darling."

Bertha and Willow crowded around him, much to the annoyance of the other women in the gym who wanted some time with him.

"We know you prefer men," Willow whispered. "And that's okay with us."

"Better than okay," Bertha said. "We can be open and honest and not worry about you trying anything."

Tomas became angry, but kept his cool, and removed their hands from his arms. "Thank you for your concern ladies, but my sexuality is no one's business. Please go back to your stations, or move on to the next." He left them and moved onto to another client.

"That went down like a lead balloon," Willow said.

"Maybe he hasn't realised it yet," Bette said. "He *is* still young. He may not have figured it out."

"But the rest of us have?" Bertha asked.

"I had a gay husband," Bette said. "So I saw firsthand what he couldn't quite figure out for himself. He's young, he'll get there."

*****

Tomas took his lunch break in the private gardens of the resort. It backed onto the beach, and staff members were allowed to use it. He sat and contemplated what the ladies had said. He'd never questioned his sexuality, never had reason to as he'd never been attracted to anyone. He just wasn't interested. As his mother said, he'd know when the right person came along. Yet clearly the right person had never come along, not that it mattered, he *was* only twenty-two. Neither Carlos nor Pedro had girlfriends. Carlos did whatever he wanted, but had no one serious, and Pedro had only recently found himself a girl, even if she was the boss's daughter. So why did *he* need to worry?

He thought about the guy he'd run into, twice, and sighed. The revelation worried him. *I'm sitting here thinking about a man and not a woman. Am I gay?*

He stopped thinking, breathing, being.

Am I gay?

Just because you have the tingles for a man doesn't make you gay, he argued with himself.

Yeah, but it's not like I've had the tingles for a woman.

True.

Suddenly the world seemed a heavy burden on his shoulders, and the weight of it on his chest made it want to collapse. Another sigh came from the pit of his stomach. Sighing was something he'd done a lot of since Carlos left. Standing, he breathed deeply and realised there was only one thing to do. Stop worrying about his brothers and start worrying about himself and his own future.

Whatever the hell that was.

*****

"Any word from Carlos or Pedro?" Tomas asked his mother when he got home.

She looked up, teary-eyed, and put the wooden spoon down. She'd been making lamb stew, but didn't have the heart to put into it. "No."

"Oh, Mama. I'm so sorry." He hugged her.

"What for? You haven't done anything." She patted his arm.

Silence.

"No," he finally said. "But I may be about to…"

She looked up with worry and surprise on her face. "What do you mean? What have you done or what are you about to do? Tell me, Tomas!"

"Mama, it's okay," he reassured her. "I haven't done anything. It's just…" He sighed yet again and leant against the kitchen counter. "With Carlos and Pedro gone, where does that leave me?" He shrugged a shoulder. "What do *I* do now?"

"You have your job, don't you love that?" She moved over to her son, sensing he was in crisis.

"I love my job at the resort, but that's just the tourist months. What about when that's over?" He shook his head and lowered his voice. "I don't want to go back to working in papa's shop over the winter. I just don't. I hate it." Tears sprang to his eyes at the thought of betraying his father by not wanting to work in the shop. "What do I do now my brothers have gone? What kind of life do I get to have?"

Jenny felt her son's pain and took him into her arms. "Oh, Tomas, my poor baby." She always knew he was different to his brothers. They were outgoing, he was not. They were boisterous, he was quiet, preferring to go about his business on his own. She had wondered when they would find nice girls and settle down, but each had preferred their lives as they were, deciding that marriage and children could wait. Now two were gone, and Tomas remained.

She stepped back. "Whatever you decide will be up to you. You don't owe your father or me anything. If you don't want to work in the shop anymore, that's fine. If you want to go and live or work somewhere else to pursue your dreams, then go. Don't feel guilty." She stroked his cheek, and he smiled. "If everything that's happened has made you question your part in life then please, *please* do whatever will make you happy."

"Even if that's leaving home?"

She put on a brave face. "Even if that means leaving home. And believe me, I know all about leaving home.

I did it for your father, so I can hardly stop my boys from doing it too."

"Didn't you feel guilty when you left Grandma and Grandpa? We certainly didn't get a say in it."

Jenny frowned. "*Of course* I felt guilty leaving my family and taking you boys away from your home, and school, and friends. And for years I fretted that I had made the wrong decision, but you all loved it here so much I never thought any of you would leave." She saddened. "Guess I was wrong."

"Oh, Mama." Tomas hugged her. "We're not boys anymore. For whatever reason Carlos and Pedro left it was clearly necessary. If I leave, it will be my choice."

"Are you thinking of leaving?" Spiros asked from the doorway, having heard snippets of conversation as he'd come in.

Tomas and Jenny looked up in surprise, and Tomas shrugged. "My brothers are gone, so what's keeping me here? Maybe I should go and see the world. Maybe go home to Australia and see my aunts and uncles and cousins." He shrugged again. "I don't know. What I do know is that maybe my time for leaving is coming."

"And what about the shop?"

"What about it?" Tomas asked. "You just hire other people."

Spiros felt his anger rise. "*But it's your legacy.* You're the only one left to work there."

"*No,* Spiros," Jenny told him. "It's *your* legacy. Your father was the reason I packed up my life and my children and moved half way around the world. He left the shop to *you, not* the boys. It's not their legacy, it's *yours* and don't tell them otherwise." She gave him the evil eye that always made him back down. "It's *your* shop, and I won't let you force them into working there if they don't want to. Are we clear?"

He knew better than to argue with his wife; the strong Aussie woman who had left everything behind and sacrificed so much for him. He backed down. He didn't like it, but knew he had to for the sake of his family. What was left of it anyway.

Jenny looked at Tomas. "If you want to go, go. We won't stop you."

Tomas looked from his father's sheepish expression to his mother's determined one and kissed her hand. "But you'll cry a lot won't you?"

"*Of course* I will. My babies have nearly all left me."

*****

Over the next few days, Tomas did a lot of thinking. Where would he go? What would he do? He hadn't planned to leave, but had a healthy bank balance from all the years of working, doing extra training on the side and under the table. He knew Carlos had made a tonne of money doing extra work and was heading for being a millionaire thanks to all those rich women he screwed for fun. But he wasn't like that. Nope, he wanted to make it without using people to do it. He'd been training, and not much else, and decided to ask the ladies what they thought.

"Oh, I think it's a brilliant idea," Bertha said Thursday

morning. "You could come to Miami and train all of the women I know. They'd pay handsomely to be told what to do by someone as gorgeous as you."

"I hadn't considered Miami," Tomas said, helping Bette with her stretches. "Lean a little more to the left," he told her as she bent. "I haven't even picked a place to go. I just know that with my brothers gone it's time to spread my wings."

"If you want somewhere that's similar to the islands then it's really only Miami or L.A. with their beaches and rich people–"

"In need of one on one attention from a hot stud like you," Bertha interrupted.

"And tropical atmosphere," Bette continued. "They might feel like home compared to anywhere else."

"I do have my native Australia to go back to. I have a lot of family there. And bend right," he told Bette.

She bent right. "But Australia is such a tiny little place when America is bursting at the seams with rich women who need to get in shape and want to pay a man to do it for them."

"What about San Francisco?" Willow asked from the floor. She was in the cobra yoga pose and went into downward dog.

"Why San Francisco?" Tomas asked.

"Well, that's where your people are." She bent into upward dog.

Tomas cocked a brow. "*My* people?"

"Don't listen to her," Bette said with a wave of her hand. "She's not all there."

"You know…gays." Willow slid into child's pose.

"As I said," Bette went on. "Don't listen to her. Come to Miami."

Tomas was frowning. "My sexuality, whatever it may be, is no one's concern."

"Of course not, dear," Bertha said. "Shut up, Willow. Come to Miami. Between the three of us, we can give you a place to stay, get you clients, and get you up and running in no time."

"That's right." Bette bent forward from the waist and touched the floor. "Between the three of us, we can get you a few hundred clients right away. And I have a huge ballroom that's not being used if you want to hold classes." She rolled into a standing position. "We could buy equipment if you need it, and when you're able to move into your own space, we'll help you set up your own gym. What do you say?"

Bertha and Willow gathered by her side.

"Oh, yes," Bertha said. "Maybe Luiz could help you out. He's a trainer."

Tomas put his hands up to stop them. "Ladies, this is all very nice and kind of you, but I haven't even decided what I'm doing, or where I'm going."

"Doesn't matter," Bette said. "The choice will be Miami. Even if we have to pack you up and take you home with us."

"Absolutely," Bertha and Willow agreed.

Tomas laughed. It had been a while since he'd done that. Laugh. "Thank you for your kindness and generosity. I will definitely think about it. Now, let's get you back to exercising."

*****

That night, Tomas had his first client of the evening. The guest had booked a two hour session of exercise and sauna. He was organising the towels and water bottles when his client walked in.

"Am I late?"

Tomas looked up to see the man from the bar and ferry. The aqua eyes were bright across the room. The tanned torso strained through the tight tank top, and his manhood strained to be released from his incredibly snug and tight exercise shorts.

The man closed and locked the door. "Don't want anyone disturbing us." He walked over to Tomas. "Hey…"

Tomas smiled despite himself and the butterflies wreaking havoc in his stomach. "Hey."

Silence.

"You booked a session…" Tomas finally said.

"Yeah. It was the only time I could get in. I have you for two hours."

Tomas blinked. "Me…" he breathed. "You have me…?" He swallowed.

"Yeah," the man breathed back. "I have you." He watched Tomas trying to get a hold of himself. "Have you even *been* with a man?" he asked softly.

Tomas breathed…and shuddered. Was a man who he wanted to be with? "No…"

"Well, I can do without the workout, so how about we get straight to the sauna?" He reached out, his fingers entwining with Tomas's as he led him to the steam room.

"I…ah…" Tomas backed up against the door. "Wait, what…?"

"Shh," the man said, putting a light finger to Tomas's lips. "We'll go slowly." He poured water on the rocks and steam filled the black tiled room.

Sweat dripped from Tomas's forehead as he watched the man slowly remove his top…up his body…over his head…onto the floor…oh, God, how he wanted the masculine…manly…male…flesh before him.

Fingers hooked into those teeny tiny shorts, and he sensually pushed them down revealing a manhood that matched the size of his own. The shorts slid to the floor. "Come." He held out a hand to Tomas, who had no control over his brain, taking his hand and guiding him to the wall near the rock box. His hands went under Tomas's tank to slide it over his head. It fell beside his own. His hands slid into his shorts and lowered them slowly, his fingers caressing Tomas's thigh muscles. The shorts fell.

"Wait…I…" Tomas breathed and grabbed the stud's hands. His insides started to freak out. What the hell was he doing? "I…I…don't…"

"You've never been with a man."

Tomas blushed, embarrassed, what for, he didn't know. "I've never been with anyone," he gasped, lightheaded and dizzy with the first stages of lust. "I just haven't found…anyone."

"There's a first time for everything," the man said. "I'll go slowly. Nothing heavy, no expectations, let me teach you. Let me *show* you…" He moved closer, nuzzling Tomas's cheek. His tongue darted out to taste him, to lick his earlobe, taste his neck. His lips moved seductively in the hollow at the back of the jaw under the ear, and Tomas groaned.

The man slid his fingers up Tomas's arms and across his broad chest. His lips made their way down his neck to his collarbone and drank the sweat that pooled there.

Tomas felt his body weaken and sag against the wall. God, he had never felt these things before, for man or woman, so why now, why with this one, why did it feel so damn good…why was he turned on? Why was he falling? Oh, God…how he was falling…

His cock was hard, the bare naked feelings catapulting themselves around his insides were new, and exciting, and daring, and he wanted all of them. He swallowed as the man's tongue, and lips and fingers made their way down to his right nipple, sucking and tasting and teasing. "Oh, God," barely came out of his mouth mixing with the whirling steam, making him light-headed in such an enclosed space.

The man greedily sucked on the nipple, his mouth moving across the hair smattered across Tomas's chest. The sweat clung, nourishing him to go on. His mouth and hands and lips moved down. Hands settled on hips, tongue settled in his navel, mouth settled in the V of his lower body. Kneeling between Tomas's legs, his fingers went into his underpants, pulled them over his erection, and down to his ankles.

"Oh," Tomas breathed in the steam. "Oh." His head went back against the wall, and he felt the man take him whole. "Oh, God…oh, God." All breath left him, and he bowed, his head falling forward to see the man between his legs capturing all of him.

The man's hands moved their way up his inner thighs, massaging, manipulating until they found what they were looking for; the precious globes either side of Tomas's manhood that had disappeared into his mouth.

Tomas slid his hands through the stud's hair and hung on. Guiding him, holding him, keeping him there, and knowing what to do without having ever done it before. It was natural and rhythmic and right. His head went back, his body arched, and he fed the man exactly what he wanted to give him.

Himself.

The man did exactly as he wanted.

Sucked.

And Tomas let him.

The twelve inches that were Tomas Giorgio Stephanopoulos was long, strong and gloriously hard and, oh, so fucking ripe for the picking.

Or sucking.

Tomas's testicles were a handful, matching the size of the penis in every way. The man held them, handled them, squeezed them to make him orgasm. He sucked more, taking it, swallowing it, making Tomas Stephanopoulos his for the taking.

Tomas arched against the wall as he came in the man's mouth. Screwing up his face at the pleasurable explosion, screwing up his hands in the man's hair to hang on and not let him go…he allowed himself a release he'd never experienced before.

He collapsed against the wall, breathing hard as the man left a trail of kisses up his penis to his torso to his neck to his lips. They kissed. Tomas had never felt the pleasure of a tongue in his mouth, let alone a man's, and he liked it. The kissing was urgent, passionate, and the man's tongue invaded, taking all of him.

The steam rose, swirled, surrounded them as they touched. The man guided Tomas's hands to him, wrapped them around him, guided him to explore. He placed his forehead against Tomas's, and they both looked down between them. Their hands greedily held and rubbed and felt. He rubbed his own against his lover's and two cocks entwined, two balls became four, and two men rubbed against each other.

Tomas had never held a man, never touched what was the same as his. The hardness, the roughness, the feel and weight of another man in his hands was exhilarating, arousing, and dangerously tempting. Dangerously tempting him to do things he had never thought of doing before. Yet he wanted to do them again and keep on doing them.

The steam rose, swirled, surrounded them as the man moved away, added more water to the rocks, and led Tomas to the bench. He laid him down and lay next to him. They kissed, explored and touched every inch of each other until the man gently rolled Tomas onto his back and rolled on top of him.

Tomas responded. Opening himself, wrapping his legs around the man. He hitched his legs up and around his waist, and without a second thought, the man entered. Tomas cringed for a moment. "Ah."

"Relax," the man soothed. "Just relax."

Tomas relaxed and felt the man rock back and forth. The rhythm, the steam, the headiness was all too much. "Oh, God," he groaned.

The man's mouth covered his, his tongue did as much damage as his penis on Tomas's nerves, sending him over the edge as the man's hand dipped down between them to take hold of the man beneath him.

They both climaxed.

They both relaxed.

The man stroked Tomas's side. He was leaning up on his elbow, his face beside his lover's. "You're gorgeous," he said. "Manly, beautiful, amazing." His fingers blazed up and down Tomas's side. "Muscular, sculptured…perfect."

Tomas felt alive. Here he was lying underneath a man, and he'd never felt so calm, so at peace. A soft smile spread across his lips. "It's genetics."

"And genetics gave you a twelve inch cock?" The man's fingers lightly swept over it, and it moved.

"More than likely." Tomas moved his fingers over his lover's. They joined. "You have a fairly healthy percentage yourself."

The man grinned. "So I've been told."

Tomas took a deep breath and slowly let it out. What a place for his first time to be in. A steam room of all places, in the resort gym. "Shit! What time is it?" He tried to check his watch, but it was fogged over. "Your two hours are probably up."

"Relax. If the next customer complains just tell

them you had a guest who needed special attention." He pulled Tomas back and kissed him.

Tomas responded and got lost once again in his new lover. Finally, though, he pulled away. "We really need to go. I have other clients." Reluctantly he sat up and grabbed a towel, wrapping it around his waist. "We'd better go." Picking up his clothes as the man grabbed his own towel, he unlocked the door. Walking into the hallway, he saw the clock read ten-ten. "Shit! Ten minutes late for my next client and I need a shower."

He heard a jangle of keys in the gym door and froze, and within seconds the manager walked in.

"I'm sure there is a reasonable explanation for him running late." He looked up and saw Tomas wrapped in a towel. "Ah, there you are, you're running late." He saw the man come out beside him wrapped in a towel as well. "I see you were in the sauna so obviously lost track of time. Try not to next time."

The man spoke up. "Sorry I kept him. I had a strenuous workout, and he helped my muscles recover in the steam room. We didn't realise what the time was. Do we have time for a shower?"

"I know that voice." Bertha stuck her head around the door. "Luiz, there you are. I've been looking everywhere for you. You should have told me you were coming for a workout, I would have joined you."

Tomas stood horrified. Not only was his manager, his boss, standing before him, but he and his new lover were standing in nothing but towels, dripping wet and holding their clothes. And now Bertha had stuck her head around the door.

"Luiz?" he asked, uncertainly, gazing at the muscle man beside him that he'd just given himself to.

"Yes. Hello, Tomas darling. Remember I mentioned my fitness trainer fiancé? Well, it's Luiz. Luiz, I see you've met Tomas, what a hunk, huh? Isn't he everything I said he was?"

The pit of Tomas's stomach fell to the floor.

"Yes," Luiz purred, laying a hand on Tomas's shoulder. "*Everything* and then some."

All Tomas wanted to do as he looked from Bertha's blank expression to Luiz's smirk was vomit.

*****

Tomas called in sick Friday morning and spent the day in bed. He was absolutely gutted that the man he had been with was his client's fiancé. How he'd managed to get through the rest of the night was still a blur, with two more clients before midnight, and he vaguely remembered stumbling home and crawling into bed where he now lay wanting to vomit.

His stomach muscles were clenched, his arms were wrapped around him, his legs curled up under him. He was in the foetal position.

"Tomas." Jenny knocked on the door. "Are you all right, sweetie?"

God, the shame. He buried his face into his pillow and tried not to sob. His first encounter with anyone had turned into his worst nightmare.

Jenny opened the door and saw him curled up which made her worry even more. Closing the door, she sat beside him. "I know something is wrong." She laid her hand on his arm. "You've never had a day off in your life."

He couldn't hold it in any longer. A sob escaped from his throat, and the floodgates opened. His body shuddered with shame, regret and pain.

"Oh, my baby." Jenny lay beside him stroking his hair, holding him close. "What is it? What's happened? Oh, my baby boy." She held him until he was finished. "Tell me what's wrong."

After a few moments, he shifted his head. His face had been buried the whole time, and now he peered out with one eye. "I can't."

"Why not?" She stroked his hair.

Silence.

"Because I'm too ashamed." He closed his eye and turned his head back to the pillow.

"Whatever it is it can't be that bad."

"It is."

"Please tell me."

With a heavy sigh, he turned his face enough to say, "I had sex last night."

Jenny's brows rose. It wasn't the first time she'd had to deal with sons having sex, but it was the first time for Tomas. "Were you safe?"

Another sigh. "I think so."

Her brows rose higher. "What *do you mean, you think so*? Did you *not* wear protection?"

"*I* didn't."

"So, you left it up to her? Women can't wear… oh…" She softened. "Tomas."

He sobbed. "I'm sorry."

"For what?"

"Being a disappointment."

Her heart broke. "Aw, sweetie, you're not a disappointment. You're only twenty-two, you're still discovering who you are and what you want to be and do." She hugged him tightly. "I always wondered why you were so quiet compared to your brothers, and then I realised you're exactly like your father. He keeps a lot of stuff in too, but it's not a *bad* thing." She kissed his cheek. "Neither is being different to others…if it's not women you're into…"

"Mama." He shifted uncomfortably.

"No, Tomas. There's nothing to be ashamed of. If you have feelings for a boy or man, then you should try to understand why. Besides, would you rather talk to your father about this?"

His head shot around to look at her. "God, no."

She smiled softly and lay back against the headboard. "I can't say I'm not disappointed, but…" Her head moved up and down as she thought, "I will support you if you want to explore…things…" She blushed. "Your sexuality with men."

His legs uncramped themselves and he spread out as he turned to her. "Really?"

Her smile widened. "Really."

His eyes closed for a moment. "Even if I stuff up royally?"

"What happened?"

He sighed and stared at the corner of the ceiling. "I saw…a man…on the beach the other day and then again coming off the ferry on Sunday. He's…" He softened. "Gorgeous. Aqua eyes I drown in…" His lips turned up at the corners. "He came into the gym last night. He'd booked a two hour session just to see me, and he took me into the sauna…" He blushed. "It was my first experience."

"And…"

The shame came back. "And when our time was up I was running late, and the manager unlocked the door and came in."

"Were you dressed?" Jenny prayed that he had been.

"Ah…" Tomas blushed deeper. "We had towels around us."

"Well, at least that's something."

"Yes, but…" Tomas made a face. "Then Bertha, one of my clients, popped her head through the doorway and that's when it all hit the fan."

"What did?"

"Bertha recognised the man I'd just been with as her fiancé Luiz," rushed out of his mouth. "Oh, God, I'm so stupid." He swung his legs around and sat on the side of the bed then shifted, as the ache of newly used muscles made him a tad uncomfortable. "The first time I'm with someone, and I don't bother getting his name or even finding out if he's attached."

"And why not? We raised the three of you better than that."

"And yet Pedro did the same thing, and Carlos beds women by the truckload without getting their names," Tomas scoffed. "I'm not the only one making stupid mistakes."

"No, you're not. But I thought *you'd* be more sensible."

His head dropped into his hands. "Ugh, so did I."

"So, what do you do now?" They had raised their sons to think for themselves, to find their own way out of the problems that were going to arise in their life. She prayed that Carlos and Pedro were doing that right now.

"I don't know," he moaned. "I had sex with an engaged man. As if having sex with a man isn't bad enough, he's engaged."

"Don't feel ashamed about the fact he's a guy. The problem is he's attached, and you didn't find out beforehand. You should talk to him, but that's your choice. You need to think long and hard about what you want with the person you want to be with. Regardless of *who* it is. If this was a mistake, admit it, own it, and move on. If you have real feelings for him, admit them, own them, and deal with the consequences. The choice is yours. I can't tell you what to do."

With another sigh, he straightened. "No. Only I can. Thanks, Mama." He leant over and kissed her on the cheek.

"Why don't you have a shower and I'll get you something to eat." Jenny squeezed his arm and went to cook up a hot breakfast, albeit a late one, and Tomas spent the rest of the day on the balcony thinking about his future.

*****

Saturday morning, Tomas took a boat to a small island

off Mykonos which had a tiny little cove that faced the endless ocean away from everyone else. After pulling the boat up on the sand, he grabbed his bag and towel and set about sunbaking for the rest of the day.

He was lying back on his towel, eyes closed and covered in shades, when he heard a motor. Lifting his head, he saw a small motorboat come into the cove and beach itself.

Luiz stepped onto the sand, waving an arm excitedly.

Tomas's heart beat faster. So did his erection.

Luiz ran to him, a broad smile on his face. "I found you."

"Why did you follow me?" Tomas sat, knees up, arms on his knees to hide his acknowledgement.

"Because I wanted to be with you." Luiz knelt in front of him. "You didn't come to work yesterday. I followed you today. I want you, Tomas. I want to be with you."

Tomas frowned at the tanned god before him. The tanned god that was making him melt in the Greek summer sun. He'd come there to think and be alone, to decide on the course of his life and not to see the man who'd so forcefully made it explode. *So not helping matters.* "Please leave. I need to spend some time alone."

"No." Luiz stood and removed his shorts, revealing his own engorged member, before kneeling again in front of Tomas, pushing his legs apart, moving between them. He took Tomas's face in his hands.

"Luiz." Tomas pulled back. "I don't want to do this. You're engaged to Bertha for Christ's sake." He pushed the hands away, leaning back to do so, and that gave Luiz the moment he needed to push Tomas onto his back, whip his shorts off, and lie on top of him.

"Luiz, what are you doing?" Tomas demanded but gave up the fight when Luiz's tongue delved into his mouth. His hands grabbed, his legs entwined, his tongue greedily attacked back.

Luiz made his way down Tomas's neck.

"Luiz, no, we can't," Tomas gasped as Luiz moved down his chest. "It's not right…you're engaged…you're…oh, God…Luiz…" He felt the warmth around him. The wet, slick mouth and its dastardly tongue. "Oh, God," he groaned and grabbed Luiz by the hair.

Luiz stayed there until Tomas came before making his way back up to cover him wholly. "Let me love you," he whispered, rubbing himself against his young lover. "I want you, Tomas."

"Oh, Luiz…I want you, too…" Tomas whispered, before being consumed with passion and desire he'd never felt before.

They stayed conjoined in the sun for hours with the tropical breeze caressing their hot, naked sun-drenched bodies until they came up for air.

"Oh, God," Tomas gasped as Luiz rolled off to lie beside him. "Oh, God."

"Oh, God indeed." Luiz stroked Tomas's stomach. "You are amazing, Tomas Stephanopoulos."

Tomas glowed in the sun. "You're pretty amazing yourself for a man who's engaged to a woman."

Luiz sighed and gazed over the ocean. "Bertha is…"

He waved his hand trying to think of the word.

"Your fiancée," Tomas finished the sentence.

"A means to an end." Luiz sighed. "I know, I know, it sounds bad," he said to Tomas's shocked expression. "But Bertha came along at a time when I didn't have a lot of clients and business wasn't going too well. So I gave her what she wanted."

"Do you do that to all rich old women?" Tomas sat up in disgust.

"No, no." Luiz sat up beside him. "Look, I…" He sighed again and scratched his head. "I've known for a few years now that I was into men. That doesn't mean I haven't been with women. I have."

"So, you're a whore," Tomas spat. "And now you've made me one."

"No," Luiz said firmly. "I'm not, and neither are you. I've been with three women and five men. You're the fifth. I first had sex with a girl at eighteen and didn't really like it. I experimented with a couple of guys, but that's all it was then, experimenting, coz we were young and naïve and had no idea how to have sex with a man. I tried again with women. But again, women didn't interest me. I met a guy, and it lasted six months, another guy lasted two years, and then there was Bertha, and now there's you. I'm crazy about you Tomas." He shook his head. "I'm crazy about you. You're gorgeous and perfect. More than any other man I've ever met or been with."

"Little comfort." Tomas snorted. "You're using a perfectly lovely woman for your own needs. Financial needs."

"And she probably knows it," Luiz said. "I've been with her a year. We don't have sex a lot, but it is companionship."

"So, what the hell is this?" Tomas spat, getting up and stalking down to the water's edge. He put his hands on his hips and stood looking out over the ocean. *How could I be so stupid?* he thought. *The first time I feel anything for anyone and it had to be the fiancé of a client. Jesus, how stupid can I be? And now I've gone and done it again.* He rubbed his face. "God how could I be so stupid." Hands slid around his waist. "Don't," he commanded.

Luiz's hands stopped at Tomas's navel. "Tomas, I didn't plan for this to happen. I didn't plan to meet someone." Lips kissed Tomas's shoulder lightly, leaving kisses along his neck. "I'm crazy about you." His right hand slid downward. "We don't have to tell anyone. We're here, in this private cove." A tongue flicked out to touch his ear. "With no one around." His fingers found what they were looking for and received a groan in return. "Tomas," he whispered. "This will be our little secret. No one will ever have to know." His hand curled around Tomas as he hardened. "Let us have today." His tongue travelled along Tomas's neck as his head fell onto Luiz's shoulder.

Tomas groaned. The man that lit a fire in him had him in the palm of his hand. The fingers worked their magic, stroking, kneading, plying up and down. The left hand stroked his stomach, lazily moving back and forth across his abdomen, dipping into his navel, stroking down to join the other hand, both of them massaging everything he was as a man. His knees were so weak he couldn't stand up any longer, and he slid into the water, Luiz right behind him, supporting his weight as he couldn't support himself.

Luiz knew he needed him; knew he had to keep him. And if this was the way to do it, by seducing him with sex, then he would. He knew how to please a man, and Tomas was the man he wanted to please. The thought of being inside of him, of having him inside took him to breaking point. And here on the deserted tropical island with no one around, he would have him.

He lowered Tomas to the sand, the water gently lapping at his thighs, and took him whole into his mouth. Tomas groaned his acceptance, and Luiz sucked harder. He rolled it around in his mouth, savouring its flavour, its length, its width. Tomas Stephanopoulos was the man he wanted in his mouth. The man he wanted his mouth around. He plied the testicles with forceful fingers until Tomas arched and groaned and he took him for all he had. Oh, yes, Tomas Stephanopoulos would never want anyone else.

*****

Tomas hadn't planned on spending the night on the island, but that's what had happened, and now it was a rush to get back home late in the afternoon. After spending all Sunday frolicking and making love, Tomas and Luiz took their boats back to Mykonos, with Tomas feeling guilty all the way.

"Weren't you supposed to be back yesterday?" Jenny asked as he came barrelling through the door all suntanned and guilty.

"What? Um, yeah." He stopped. "Um…I ended up staying, took the time to sort some stuff out." He inched his way toward the bedrooms.

"Go and have a shower," Jenny told him, knowing something had happened. "Dinner will be ready soon."

Tomas raced for his room, got his bag ready for the next day and hit the shower, strolling out just as his mother served dinner.

"So…what did you decide?" Jenny asked, handing a bowl of salad to him.

Tomas looked from her to his father before taking some salad and passing the bowl on. "About what?"

"About staying here or travelling?" Jenny laughed. "What did you think I meant?" She saw his guilty look. "Oh, you do have other things on your mind."

"Like what?" Spiros asked, picking up a lamb chop. "What's going on in my son's mind?"

Tomas gulped. This wasn't going to be easy. "Well…" He wiped his sweaty palms on his shorts. "If my plan goes through, I thought of travelling to America. Seeing the sights."

"That would be nice. Anywhere in particular?" Jenny popped a cherry tomato into her mouth.

"Miami," Tomas said. "The ladies at the gym have gone on and on about it, with its beaches and sun. It sounds like a great place to go."

"If it's beaches and sun you want, we have that

here." Spiros waved his fork. "We live on an island for God's sake."

"But it's not America," Tomas said, shrugging a shoulder. "I want to visit other countries and cultures."

"Mmm," Spiros mumbled, jamming lettuce into his mouth. "Pah, other cultures."

"*Yes*, other cultures. They *are* half Australian remember." Jenny eyed him. "So don't 'pah other cultures'." She imitated his gesture.

"Mmm." Spiros finished up. "I'm going to Mikado's for a drink." He left them to it.

Jenny sighed, hating that Spiros went off for a drink every Sunday night instead of spending it with his family. But he had insisted on doing it, and no woman was going to stop him. He'd received an evil eye for that one, but she had allowed him to do it since he was home every other night. Once the door was shut she moved in. "What else happened this weekend? Did you see him?"

Tomas reddened.

"Tomas." She frowned. "He's engaged."

"I know, I know," he wailed. "I couldn't help it." Looking plaintively at the ceiling he continued. "I was there on my own, and then he turns up and says he followed me and one touch and a kiss later I'm putty in his hands." He closed his eyes in embarrassment. "Literally."

"Aw, sweetie." She reached over and patted his hand. "What are you going to do? Do you love him, or is it just some kind of first-time attraction?"

"Love?" Tomas's eyes flew open. "No...I..." He

shook his head slowly, trying to decipher his emotions. "Not…love…just…"

"Pure unadulterated lust," Jenny finished with a raised brow.

His blush deepened. "Yes."

"So, what are you going to do?"

His deep sigh came out slowly. "Confess to my crime."

*****

Monday morning, after a guilt-filled gym session, Tomas pulled Bertha aside. "My dear Bertha, there is something I need to confess and apologise for."

"Oh, darling, what do you have to apologise for?"

Bette and Willow gathered round.

Tomas glowed red with shame. "I've done something that is unforgivable, and I'm sorry."

"For what? What could you have possibly have done?" Bertha asked.

"I met a man," Tomas said softly.

"Oh, how wonderful," Bette cried. "Tell us all about it."

"But why would you need to apologise to me for that?" Bertha asked, confused.

The shame was too much of Tomas. "I first saw him at the beach bar last week and then on the ferry. I didn't know who he was, but he tracked me down to the gym and seduced me." He stared, shamefaced, at the floor. "He made me feel things I've never felt before, and I let things happen, and I shouldn't have, and, dear Bertha, I need you to forgive me. It will never happen again." He took her hands, his eyes pleading.

"But why do I need to forgive you, Tomas?" Bertha asked, her silky kaftan wafting around her ankles. "I don't understand any of this and what I have to do with you meeting a man."

"Because I did not know the man's name until you said it, dear Bertha. Said it in the gym Thursday night." He swallowed, his face crumpling up with the pain of guilt he was feeling. "I'm so, so sorry."

"Thursday night?" Bertha asked slowly, completely bewildered. "What happened Thursday…oh…you mean when I found you with Luiz…oh…oh, dear Tomas."

"I am so sorry, Bertha," he sobbed at her changing expression. "I didn't know he was Luiz, your Luiz. He never told me his name and I stupidly never asked. Please forgive me for I have done very bad things. Please, please forgive me." Tears flowed down his face, burning his flesh with shame and guilt.

Bertha's heart went out to the poor boy. She knew about Luiz's sexual past and knew it would possibly happen again. "Do you feel you've been taken advantage of?"

He swallowed the big fat lump of guilt in his throat. "Yes. Especially over the weekend when he followed me out to one of the islands and had his way with me," he choked. "I told him I'd never been with anyone and…" He closed his eyes in shame. "I let him do that to me anyway. I couldn't stop him, even if I wanted to. I am so sorry, Bertha. Please, please forgive me. I'm begging you."

Bette and Willow stared from Tomas to each other to Bertha. They had never seen a man cry over being gay and taking a lover, but clearly, Tomas was a sensitive young soul still learning about the ways of life, love, and gay sex.

"Oh, Tomas," Bertha said, patting his hand. "It's perfectly okay. If he was going to screw anyone, at least it was you."

Tomas looked up under swollen hooded eyes. "But I—"

She shook her head. "I knew he was gay, he told me and was very honest about it from the beginning. He'd had sex with men *and* women, but he was hot, and I was lonely, and he's very good at what he does, isn't he?"

Tomas blushed at the memories.

"Don't worry about it. At least he has good taste." She laughed. "We both do."

"But I—"

"I know," she said. "You had sex with an engaged man." She gave a woeful nod. "A *gay* engaged man, but I knew what I was in for and probably knew when I brought him here that *someone* would come along. Of course, someone *would*, the place is full of beautiful young bodies. But that's not going to stop me from making you come to Miami. Now, we've been thinking—"

"But, Bertha." Tomas shook his head in confusion at the sudden change of subject. "I slept with your fiancé. That is unforgivable. What I did was so wrong." His guilt and shame was eating him up inside, and he felt himself withering away as he was being eaten.

"Tomas, there is nothing to forgive," she said, trying to make him understand. "End of discussion. I don't hate you, I don't want you dead." She watched his expression rise and fall. "Stop feeling ashamed for finding love or some form of it. If being with him made you happy then so be it. Maybe we can share him, or, maybe it's time for me to get a younger fiancé." She laughed. "But back to you. We want you to come to Miami. We want to help you out and introduce you to our friends. Say you'll come."

Bette laid a bejewelled hand on his arm. "Please say you'll come."

"But I have not been very kind to you," he told Bertha. "I'm sick just thinking about what I have done."

"Then stop feeling sick," Bertha demanded. "It's done, it's over, because what's done cannot be undone, and anyway…I was just with him for companionship. Sex was only in the beginning and ended quite quickly. I'm not really into that sort of thing anymore, so I paid him to stick around. He wines me and dines me, travels with me, and I show him off to my friends. Tomas…" She touched his cheek. "I really don't care if he slept with someone. But I *am* glad he picked you. Now, stop looking confused and be done with the infidelity. It means nothing and is no big deal. *We* have been talking and want you to come to Miami with us."

Tomas swallowed and the lump in his throat shrunk. "And Luiz?"

"Well," Bertha said. "We either keep him or get rid of him. I'm not fussed either way, but if you want a fresh start without guilt…say you'll come to Miami."

"Yes, say you'll come," Bette and Willow echoed.

August 1977

On the first of August, Tomas stepped off the private plane of Bette Olander onto the tarmac at Miami Airport.

It was a beautiful bright day with not a cloud in the turquoise blue sky as the sun shone down, layering the world in a warm, soft glow.

Tomas turned his face up toward that sun, feeling its warmth radiate on his face. He breathed the salty air drifting across on the gentle coast winds.

"Does it feel different?" Bette asked

"To what?" He looked at her in her bejewelled kaftan and kitten heels.

"To Mykonos, darling," Bette said, taking her handkerchief from her clutch and dabbing at her face. "It's still very warm."

"Well, it is still summer," Bertha said from beside her as their luggage was transferred from the plane to Bette's limo. "Of course it's going to be hot."

The driver held the back door open and they piled

in, with Tomas taking the window seat.

"You're going to love it here," Willow told him, adjusting her own bejewelled kaftan. They were all the rage that summer and all of her friends wore them as well, so she didn't care that Bette and Bertha had them on. Everyone else had them on too. "It's just like Mykonos only more glamorous."

"The night life is amazing," Bertha added, sitting in her own kaftan and bejewelled headpiece. She glanced at Bette and Willow. The three of them were like queens of the ocean in their frothy creations.

Driving down the coast to Coral Gables they rolled through extravagantly wealthy neighbourhoods with magnificent mansions behind iron gates. They came to a stop in front of one of them.

Tomas's eyes widened as they stopped at the front door. "This is your house, Bette? It's beautiful." He gazed across the expansive white home with its four round pillars, balcony, and white railings. Lush green lawns spread across the plantation-style grounds.

"Thank you, darling. Now come, I want you to see the ballroom. It faces the back, so it has an amazing view of the backyard and gardens with French doors that open all the way." She led him through the front door. "Thank you, Webster," she told the butler who'd opened the door and taken her things. She conducted everyone through the large entrance hall and opened a door on their right. A huge ballroom extended through the whole side of the house from front to back with French doors that folded back against the walls. "Webster, grab the door for me." Bette opened them and slid one side back while Webster opened the other.

They all stood looking across the terrace onto the gardens with their waterfalls and ponds, and onto the emerald lawn beyond.

"What do you think?" Bette turned around and moved to the centre of the room, waving her hands as she spoke. "We could get some equipment in and place it over that side near the front and leave this part for working out and stretching. We could do aerobics and yoga here." She spun around, clasping her hands to her chest. "Don't you just love it?"

"Oh, absolutely." Willow walked over. "It's perfect, and the cool breeze will keep us cool for the rest of summer."

"It's the perfect room," Bertha said. "Lots of space for everyone. That's if we even end up exercising. We may all just want to look at Tomas."

He heard her and blushed, and was glad he was still gazing out over the beautiful gardens so they couldn't see the glint of shame that flew over his face. It still made him uncomfortable, being around Bertha.

Cheating with her fiancé made him feel guilt so huge it would probably never subside. They had both decided to say goodbye to Luiz. Tomas made that choice on the grounds he was a mistake. He wanted to start fresh in a new town. Bertha had finally decided she wanted a man that wasn't gay.

Luiz had cried, getting down on his knees, begging to be forgiven and taken back. "Tomas, please, I love you, please, don't let me go. You're the only one I want.

I can fix it with Bertha so we can be together. You and me, just us, just here. We can live together here on Mykonos," Luiz had pleaded as he knelt before Tomas that past Saturday when he had been told it was over. *"Take me back. Don't let this stop us from being together. Don't let my past with Bertha stop us from being together. I love you, Tomas. For me, you are the one. The only one. The one I want to spend the rest of my life with. I have chosen who I want, and it is you, Tomas."*

It tore Tomas apart inside, killing off each little blood vessel that filled his heart. His first experience at love had to end in mind-numbing heartbreak.

Luiz had pleaded with both of them.

Both of them had said no; one more efficiently than the other.

They needed a clean break and what happened in Mykonos stayed in Mykonos. Luiz had been told to find his own way home and that his things would be packed and waiting for him when he returned.

"Thinking about our gigolo?" Bertha laughed daintily, noticing Tomas's faraway gaze as she floated over to him. "Don't worry, it's a fresh start for both of us, and don't you know, Miami is the new spot to be for men hooking up with men. So we'll have to get you out and about." She laid a gentle hand on his arm.

Tomas's blush deepened, and he took Bertha's hand in his and gave it a soft squeeze.

"Oh, yes," Bette said. "With all of the people we know you'll be hooked up in no time."

"I don't know." Tomas shook his head. "With the

mess I've just gotten myself out of I'm not sure I want to get into another one."

"Nonsense," Bertha said. "We'll help you find a nice boy to be with. Now, let's figure out what we need here so we can get started."

With Tomas to guide them, they spent the next hour figuring out what equipment they would need and where they could put it. One phone call and five minutes later they had bought that equipment from a store and it was being delivered that afternoon.

"What's next?" Bette asked. "Ah yes, new workout clothes for you. We'll have to take you shopping tomorrow."

He shook his head in disbelief. "I…this is too much. You have done so much for me, I can't even begin to repay you or thank you. I don't know how I'll *ever* pay you back."

Bette waved a hand. "With all the women that will want to come, I'll charge them per hour, and we'll make our money back in no time."

"Oh, yes," Bertha said. "I've already called Marina to tell everyone. They're all on board."

"And I've called Sandra to let her know, so the grapevine is in full swing. You're going to be busy all day, every day," Willow added.

Tomas's brows rose. "*All* day, every day? Seven days a week?"

Bette laughed. "Well, not seven days a week, but some of the ladies like to be early morning and some late evening. We can set up a schedule once you've met them and find out what their needs are. In the meantime, we'll show you the sights and get you settled."

Half an hour later, Tomas was in the guest room overlooking the back garden and wondering how the hell he'd managed to get there. His family had fallen apart, and now all he had left was a group of three wise ladies to guide him. He unpacked his suitcase and carry-on bag, hanging his few clothes in the closet. *I'll have to get some more of those now I'm here. Especially since it's still summer and I'm in need of new clothes,* he thought.

That afternoon, they were waiting when the workout equipment arrived and spent an hour putting it in place and setting it up.

Finally, at four-thirty, they collapsed in the garden chairs on the back terrace while Webster served iced tea.

Bette held hers up. "To Tomas, to new ventures, to new *adventures,* and a new life."

"To Tomas."

That evening, they cruised through the city and dined at *Flair et Saveur,* an expensive restaurant where only the rich dined, feasting on lobster and caviar, washing it down with Cristal champagne. After dinner, they went to *Sexe et Faveurs,* a mature club that catered for people over forty; *wealthy* people over forty who wanted pretty, *very* young things to play with. In *every* sexual manner.

The club was low key, with dimmed lights, a cool and casual but tasteful décor of oriental carpet and red walls, and lustfully decadent desserts of all kinds.

Tomas wandered after the ladies and saw young blonde things chatting up older men, and young men chatting up older ladies. There were even a few same on same meetings going on, with young hot boys kissing and groping older men, and older women getting it on with young girls.

"We're very discreet here," Bertha told him as they took their seats. "No tales ever walk out that door, and no one breathes a word about it. What do you think?"

"Mmm." Tomas looked around. "It's not really my thing. But clubs of any kind don't really interest me."

"How do you expect to meet anyone?" Willow asked, adjusting her sparkling diamond bracelet.

"I don't," Tomas replied, catching the eye of the young thing on an old man's knee across the room.

"Don't what?" she asked.

"Don't expect to meet anyone," he told her, glancing away from the couple across the room. "After Mykonos and everything that happened, I'm going to take my time, get a feel for the place and my new job, and then we'll see if I want to meet anyone."

"You need to get back on the horse darling." Bette patted his hand. "We'll make sure to introduce you to a lot of young men we know and let all the girls know to rally their troops as well."

Tomas laughed lightly, but then noticed someone walking toward him and stopped in a heartbeat. His life fell before his eyes. "Go away." His voice broke. "We told you goodbye."

Luiz came to their table. "Tomas," he pleaded and nodded to the others. "Bertha."

"Luiz," she said stiffly.

"Tomas please, I must talk to you." He knelt beside

his ex-lover, his fingers sliding over his hand. "I love you, please, I want to see you, and I *need* to be with you."

Tomas pulled his hand away. "Please leave. I don't want to see you." His discomfort was felt and seen by everyone at the table, *and* in the club. All eyes were on them, and it was embarrassing.

"Tomas," Luiz pleaded once more.

"You heard him, Luiz," Bertha cut him off. "Leave." She clicked her fingers at someone, and two burly men in suits came to their table and stood on either side of Luiz. Taking his arms, they hauled him to his feet.

"Please, Tomas, I love you. I want to be with you. We need to talk," he yelled as he was carried away. "I want you back."

"Jesus," Tomas muttered. "I didn't think he'd follow me again." He glanced around at the other patrons, staring in distaste or curiosity. "Can we leave? That was embarrassing."

"Of course. Let's go to *The Joy Stick*. It will be much better than this," Bertha said, ushering the others out of the booth.

They made their way outside and waited while the driver got their limo. Fifteen minutes later, they walked into the club to blaring music, flashing lights, and people of all races, colours and creeds.

"Oh, I love this place. You can be so free here," Willow squealed and excitedly clapped her hands before wafting away in her gold lamé kaftan. She twirled around in circles in the middle of the dance floor, the lights reflecting off the lamé making her a human disco ball. The people around her cheered.

Tomas felt someone grab his hand and turned to see Bertha intent on leading him up a small flight of stairs to a seating area. They joined a small group of women all dressed to the nines and middle-aged or older.

"Violet, Marie, Beatrice, this is Tomas, from Mykonos. The personal trainer we were telling you about." Bertha swung him around and he fell onto the couch next to Violet.

"Hello," he said, straightening himself.

"Hello," the three women said together, all eagerly eyeing off the hot new thing in their lives.

"Are you ladies friends of Bette and Bertha?" He eyed the hungry women laden with the riches of their wealth and status.

"Yes, we are," Violet said, smoothing her salt and pepper hair. The bun was surrounded in crystals that matched the choker at her throat and the bracelet on her wrist. At sixty-four she was in desperate need of a healthy young man and had demanded that the girls bring their new acquisition home from Mykonos. When they'd called to say they were, she couldn't stand the wait.

Tomas felt like a piece of meat. They were salivating, licking their lips while eyeing him hungrily, and he was the sacrificial lamb.

"So, you're going to be our personal trainer?" Beatrice sipped her champagne. At forty-five she was the youngest of their group of friends and was on to husband number three. But now she had the Greek god before her she was wondering if she should make him husband number four. Or just take him on as a lover. She crossed her legs slowly, hoping to show him she wore no underwear, and maintained eye contact. He didn't flinch and kept his eyes on hers, nowhere else.

"Why don't you go and mingle," Bette said over the music. "Relax, have fun, go fly a kite with Willow."

Tomas smiled. "I think I might." He knew he was being offered a way out and gladly took it. Walking back to the dance floor, he took the circuitous route. He wasn't quite dressed for the place; his black suit and unbuttoned matching shirt were a touch too formal for the crowd, but he looked hot, and the crowd noticed.

Men and women eyed the hot hunk of Greek man meat that casually strolled around them, hands in pockets, eyes on the lookout. Tomas felt the vibrations through the soles of his shoes. Felt them reverberate through to his bones. Clubs weren't his thing, but this one…this one was different.

He watched the people. They had no inhibitions; they just let themselves be free. Free to dance the way they wanted, dress the way they wanted, express themselves the way they wanted.

He walked past a couple of men in leather chaps and not much else, kissing against a wall. Not far from them were two women, and not far from them were two people fucking. *Clearly, anything goes in this place*, he thought as he completed the circuit.

He stood watching Willow swirl around and made his way through the crowd that seemed to part just for him. Eyes stared, hands reached out to touch, and he found his way to Willow's side.

"Tomas, darling," she panted. "Don't you just love it here? You can be so free." She twirled. "I love it, I love it, I love it."

He closed his eyes and let his body relax, getting into the rhythm of the music. Pedro had the natural beat in the family, but he could feel what Pedro used to go on about for hours. If you just relax and let it take you away, you can dance.

He swayed, he rocked, he grooved and let the music take him away.

"You didn't tell me he could dance," Violet told Bertha. "He's got rhythm besides gorgeous looks."

"I didn't know," Bertha said. "I've never seen him dance. I've seen his brother Pedro, though; he's a gorgeous boy. And the eldest, Carlos; my, how he knows how to pleasure a woman. I just didn't know about Tomas's dancing."

"So, rhythm runs in the family," Violet said, sipping her champagne.

"It definitely seems to," Bertha said, watching Tomas sway his way around the dance floor. The crowd parted for him and Willow as they sashayed to the music.

"He's hot. What does he do besides personal training?" Marie asked. She was head of an all-female law firm that dealt with the wealthy women of Florida. At fifty-nine she was one of the richest women in the state and had acquired her wealth without the help of a husband.

"Besides men you mean?" Bette mischievously winked.

"Oh." Marie's face fell. "He's a fag? What a waste."

"True," Bette agreed. "But that means you get attention and not just a man wanting to get in your pants for your money. Besides, he's a very good trainer. Just you wait and see."

"When do we start?" Beatrice asked.

"Next week," Bette replied and knocked back her fifth glass of champagne.

Violet had been thinking after Bette's reply. "He's into men…?"

"Yes," Bertha said.

"Has he ever done movies?"

"Not that I know of." Bertha eyed her friend. "What are you thinking?"

"You know Marcus is into making movies, and, of course, it's big business, especially, same on same."

"I still can't believe you're in business with your ex," Beatrice said. "Most of us can't stand our exes, or to be around them once they're gone."

"When you're in business and making a motza you want to *stay* in business," Violet replied. "It's become big in the gay scene to have same-sex movies. And if he's into men…"

"Are you going to ask him?" Marie asked.

"Who, Marcus?" Violet asked.

"No, Tomas," Marie replied.

"Oh." Violet blushed. "Yes, I guess I should ask if he'd be interested."

Tomas twirled Willow around and spied a hot looking guy over her shoulder. He looked away, not interested in getting involved again, but quickly looked back anyway. The man was standing at the edge of the crowd watching with everyone else. His dark hair was slicked back, his black shirt opened to the waist revealing a light covering of hair. He had a three-piece white suit on, á la Tony Manero from *Saturday Night Fever*, and dark eyes that couldn't take themselves off Tomas.

Tomas turned, swinging Willow in another direction, so he didn't feel the connection from those eyes. *Not again. Please God, not again, he thought. One attraction to a man is enough. I don't need to get involved with another so soon.*

"How gay is he?" Violet asked the girls.

"What?" Bertha choked on her drink and patted herself down.

"How gay is he?" Violet repeated, her eyes not leaving Tomas on the dance floor. "A little gay, a lot gay?"

"Well, I..." Bertha shook her head as the others looked on in amusement. "Didn't think you *could be* a little or a lot gay. Gay is gay."

"What I meant was, is he just *realising* he's gay, so inexperienced in the field of gayness and gay sex, or has he been fucking his own kind for years?"

"Oh," Bertha said. "That's what you meant. He's only had the one experience and that was with my ex-fiancé."

"What!" Three stunned faces swivelled in her direction.

She sighed and revealed all. "I knew Luiz had been with men, I knew he would possibly pick up while on holiday. I just didn't know it was going to be with my personal trainer. The poor boy was so upset about it when he realised who Luiz was that he apologised profusely. What can I do?" She shrugged a shoulder. "It is what it is, and we have ditched Luiz for good."

"So, he's only had the one experience," Violet murmured. "Fresh meat."

"He's only *been* with one man. I don't know how many experiences," Bertha said and turned her head to watch Tomas. "It's such a pity." She sighed.

"He would be new to the whole thing. We could work on that angle. Have him play a poor boy that is taken advantage of. Do the whole, first time thing," Violet said. "Yes, yes, that would be a very good angle."

Tomas turned, straight into the path of the man in the Tony Manero suit. Their eyes met, the fire ignited, and a stunned Tomas turned again, this time heading for the bar. He wasn't a big drinker, but he needed a beer and knocked one back in five seconds flat then ordered a second.

"You're a great dancer. Do you take lessons?" the voice beside him said.

Tomas turned to see the Tony Manero lookalike.

Tony Manero grabbed a beer and leant on the bar.

"What?" Tomas said, dazed.

"Have you been taking lessons?" Tony lookalike repeated, his lips turning into a small smile.

Those lips turned Tomas on. "Uh," he muttered, looking down at the bar. "No."

"Well, you're great. Hey, have you ever been on *American Band Stand,* or one of those shows as a dancer in the background? You'd be great."

"Um." Tomas shook his head. "No. Never been on

a show." *Be cool, just be cool,* he told himself. *Don't make a fool of yourself, just be cool. No expectations. Nothing. Just be cool.*

"How about movies? You ever been in a music clip?" Tony went on.

"Ah, no. No music clips either."

"Mmm, well if you need a job, I could get you into the scene. A buddy of mine is a music producer and does music clips. He could always use extras."

"That…ah…" Tomas knocked back another beer. "Sounds good."

"I'm Roger."

"What?" Tomas finally turned to look at the tall hunk of man beside him.

"I'm Roger. Roger Dencott." The Tony lookalike was holding out his hand.

Tomas stared from the hand to the deep dark eyes that he started drowning in. *Play it cool, Stephanopoulos. Play it cool.* He started backstroking. "Tomas." Shaking hands, he felt tingles go roaring up his arm.

"Nice to meet you…Tomas," Roger said, hanging on a few moments more, feeling the tingle race up his arm and across his body. "Let me give you a card." He reluctantly let go to dig a business card out from his pocket. "This is my friend, get yourself along to a recording and you'll be in a film clip."

Tomas took the card, never once taking his eyes off Roger.

"Well, look at that." Violet held her glass up in the direction of the bar. "Our young ingénue has met my other star."

The women turned to look and watched Tomas and Roger talk.

"That's good isn't it?" Marie asked. "If he gets to know them away from work he may not be so uncomfortable *at* work."

"Yes, very good idea, Marie," Violet said. "But I certainly didn't plan this. Looks like Tomas caught Roger's eye all on his own."

"So, what do you do?" Roger asked, leaning an elbow on the bar and taking in the full length of the dark, brooding man before him; a dark, brooding man who had taken his fancy and turned him on.

"Personal trainer." Tomas was feeling relaxed now, and he should after three beers. He casually glanced at the man beside him, and those tingles kept going, and going and going on down to his groin, stirring him.

Roger studied his face. "You're not from here, though?"

"No, Mykonos. I've just come over. Landed today actually."

"Ah, then you'll need a chaperone to get you around Miami." Roger took a swig of beer, wanting it to be Tomas sliding down his throat instead of the amber fluid.

"Ah." Tomas laughed lightly. "I have three of those. What about you? What do you do?" He finished off his beer and turned around to lean on the bar so he faced the crowd.

"I'm an actor. I also help out with the setup and production of the movie. Lights, cameras, etc."

"Cool." Tomas nodded. "Anything I would have seen you in?"

Roger grimaced. He wasn't sure if the hot-looking stud was even gay considering he'd turned up with three older women. He could just be a gigolo. "Well, unless you've seen *Hunk on Hunk, Hot Balls,* or *Big Dick* then probably not."

The titles bounced around in Tomas's brain. "Oh, my God." His eyes closed and he bowed his head. "Are they…gay…movies?"

"Porn, yes."

Tomas kept his eyes closed, scared to even open them. "You're a gay porn star?"

"Yes."

Ah, Jesus!

*****

"So, we saw you talking to a young man in the club last night," Bette said Tuesday morning.

They had been working out for an hour after taking an hour to warm up and get their act together. There were fifty women in Bette's ballroom, each paying ten dollars an hour to have a session with their latest Greek stud acquisition. Tomas had given each woman special attention, and now they were sorting out a schedule with Bertha.

"I was," he replied, wiping himself with a towel. "This is an amazing turnout. Thank you so much for this. If it weren't for you ladies, I wouldn't have a head start on a business."

"Don't worry about it." Bette laid a hand on his arm. "With this turnout, the equipment will be paid for at the end of the week, and then you'll start getting your share." That's the agreement they had come up with. The equipment would be paid for before they got a wage. Tomas had insisted on buying his own clothes and car, having saved a lot from his years at the resort, and insisted on paying board while he lived there so Bette would keep a portion of the income until he was set up in his own home and business.

"So…who was that young man at the bar? You were talking quite closely."

"Not really." He stepped away to grab a glass of juice from the refreshment table.

She followed. "Were you not interested?"

"Nope."

"Not interested because you're not ready for another relationship?"

"Just not interested."

"And what does he do?"

"He's an actor."

"In movies?"

"In gay porn." Tomas handed her a glass of juice. "He's a porn star."

Bette's brows rose. "Well, *it is* a well-known gay club so it was obvious that anyone you spoke to besides us, would be gay."

"I don't have a problem with talking to gay people. But he's in porn."

"Have you seen a porn movie?" Violet asked from beside them. She had come over just seconds before and heard the conversation.

Tomas sighed. "No."

"Do you know the industry is huge? *Especially* gay porn."

"No."

"Maybe you should come by the studio sometime." She fished a business card from her purse. "My ex and I run a very lucrative gay movie business, very tasteful, very classy, none of this hot horny fucking stuff. The actors in our movies make sweet love, and they are *massive* sellers. You should come along and have a look. Maybe you'll like something you see…or *someone*." She touched Bette on the arm. "I have to go. I'll see you both tomorrow. Bye Tomas."

"Violet." He looked down at the card. *Seralift Productions. Movies for All Kinds. Marcus and Violet Seralift.*

The other ladies wandered over to say goodbye and to thank Tomas for their workout. He kissed their hands and thanked them for coming, leaving them giggling like schoolgirls reliving some fantasy.

Once they were gone, Bette broached the subject again. "And what was wrong with the young man you talked to?"

"Nothing." Tomas busied himself wiping down the equipment.

"It wouldn't hurt for you to get out and about on your own. Meet people, see new places, make friends."

"I know." He dumped the towels into the laundry basket for Webster. "I'm just…" He sighed and rubbed his forehead. "Not ready to get involved."

"Who said anything about getting involved?" Bette asked. "Go out and make friends. Go and see Violet and watch a movie being made. It might make you feel more comfortable with your sexuality."

He flashed a glare at her. *What is it with other people going on about my sexuality? Why can't they just leave it to me to figure out?* "I'll think about it," he finally said.

*****

The week was full of sessions. Tomas took individual clients in the morning, and small groups of five in the afternoons. He started at eight and finished at six. He saw Violet and Bette talking on Friday morning after the workout and got a wave from Violet as she left. "What was that about?" he asked.

"She's invited us to watch a movie being made tonight at the studio. Would you like to go? See what it's all about?"

"I don't know." Tomas backed up. "It's not something I'm into."

"Oh, come on, you're in a new place to have new experiences," she cajoled. "You might learn something new about yourself."

*****

At seven that night, they drove up to the large iron gates of *Seralift Productions* and were escorted through winding roads to the studio. There was a huge sound stage with several scenarios set up in several rooms with the current one being played out in a steam room.

The moment Tomas saw the set he backed up. "No, no, I don't need to relive that moment."

Bette grabbed his arm. "Get over it, Tomas. What happened, happened. Deal with it. Now let's stay and watch."

They stood at the back of the studio watching as steam was pumped into the room and crew ran around adjusting lights and cameras.

Bette spied Violet and went off to see her, leaving Tomas alone and against the back wall.

One of the crew walked past, but stopped and turned. "Hey. I thought it was you. What are you doing here?" He saw Tomas's terrified look and began to worry. "It's Roger," he reminded him, "from the club last week. Are you okay?"

Tomas stared at the ordinary-looking guy before him. He had on jeans and a t-shirt with unstyled dark brown hair that curled around his ears and brushed his jawline. He didn't look like the actor he'd claimed to be. And he certainly didn't look like Tony Manero anymore. "I thought you said you…"

"I am." Roger smiled. "But I'm not in every movie, so I help out on others. I'm fixing lights today. How come you're here?" He couldn't stop the slow burning stirrings in his pants and hoped it wasn't too obvious. This one seemed young and inexperienced. He needed smooth, calm nudging in the right direction. And that would be *his* direction if he had any say in the matter.

Tomas blinked and relaxed, unwinding his arms

from around himself. "I came with Bette, a friend of Violet's." He nodded in their direction. "She invited us."

Roger glanced over his shoulder briefly. "Cool. You'll get to see how a movie's made."

"Yeah." Tomas let out a gush of air. "I'm not into this sort of thing."

"You don't have to be into the content, but it's fun to see a movie being made." Roger wanted to ask what was wrong, why he was so tense and wound up, but knew Tomas would need to reveal that in his own time. And he had a feeling that big secret was what was stopping the Greek stud from letting himself go.

"Yeah, whatever," Tomas muttered, hearing steam being pumped onto the set. The panic rose. "I need some air." He turned and bolted, not knowing where he was going and not actually caring, as long as it was away from the scene that reminded him of the biggest mistake of his life.

Roger followed, bouncing along lightly like Pepé Le Pew stalking his prey.

Tomas made it to the other end of the studio into an empty bedroom scene. Seeing no one around, he collapsed onto the bed and gasped for air.

"Are you okay?" Roger came up to stand beside the bed. "Does this *really* make you sick? Is it being *gay* that makes you sick?" He stared down at the very confused and anguished face before him.

Tomas gulped air, and a sob came out. "I don't know."

Roger let out a deep breath and sat beside the

forlorn figure on the bed. "*Are* you gay?"

Tomas moved his head back and forth. "I…I… don't really know."

"So, it's all new to you, then?"

Tomas nodded. "Yeah."

"Okay, that's…that's okay. Coming out is hard. Figuring out you're gay is harder. It took me five years."

Tomas finally looked at him. "For what?"

Roger shrugged a shoulder. "Everything. Figuring out I wasn't interested in girls. Thinking that meant I was interested in boys. Trying to sort out my *emotional* feelings on top of sorting out my *sexual* feelings. And when I finally let go of everyone else's expectations, I realised I was actually gay. How long's it been for you?"

Tomas hugged himself tighter and sighed. "Just… last month."

"Wow, you *are* new to this. No wonder you seem confused."

"It's not just that."

"Wasn't a good experience?"

"No."

"Yeah." Roger nodded. "Had those." He inspected Tomas's profile. "How old are you?"

"Twenty-two."

"Jesus, still so young. I remember being twenty-two; wasn't all that good for me either."

"It's not that it wasn't good." Tomas shifted uncomfortably. "It's just…he was the right guy at the wrong time and…" He broke off.

"It was your first?"

Tomas nodded. His throat was now too clenched to speak.

"Did he take advantage of you?"

Tomas remained silent, his frown deepening.

"Did he rape you?" Roger's blood boiled. How dare anyone take advantage of such a sweet young kid!

Tomas looked up in alarm, and his throat unclenched. "What? No, no, it was nothing like that. No, nothing like that at all."

"Then why are you so cut up about it?" Roger was confused. If he hadn't been forced, then it was consensual, but something was going on inside the man he wanted to get to know.

"Long story short." Tomas sighed. "I bumped into him twice at the resort I worked at, and he seduced me in the steam room, and then I found out he was the fiancé of one of my clients. A *female* client."

"Ouch!" Roger felt like laughing and crying at the same time.

"Yep."

"And now we're making a steam room movie."

"Yep."

"Brings back memories."

"Oh, yeah." Tomas nodded. "Good *and* bad."

"So, your first experience was in a steam room. How do you feel about sex with men?" Roger's insides went tight at the thought of being in a steam room with Tomas. It was definitely something he would change for the better. Give him new and improved memories of it.

Tomas looked at him strangely.

"It makes you gay," Roger said.

Tomas looked away. "I've never been attracted to girls. Never wanted to kiss one, have sex with one. But I never felt anything for boys either. I just felt… nothing," he barely whispered. "And all of a sudden I fall head over heels for a guy I didn't know, and I let him…do those things that felt so good…" His eyes closed and his voice drifted away. "It was *so* good."

"It is with the right person."

"He *wasn't* the right person. He was taken, and now it's over, and our lives could have been wrecked. It was my fault. *My* fault for not asking his name. *My* fault for being with a man I didn't know." His head dropped into his hands. "I still feel so guilty about it."

"Everyone does stupid shit they feel guilty about." Roger slapped him on the back. "You ain't no different."

Tomas heard it. He lifted his head and looked at Roger. "Did I just detect a hint of Australian accent?"

Roger's eyes widened in surprise. "How did you…?"

"I was born there." Tomas grinned. "My mother's Australian, my father's Greek. He immigrated in 1950, met mama, and then had my brothers and me. We moved to Mykonos ten years ago when I was twelve."

Roger was charmed by the Australian boy beside him. "Yeah, where were you born?"

"Armidale," Tomas said, now fully relaxed. "We grew up there until we moved back."

"How come you moved from Aus to some Greek island?" Roger was intrigued. Being Aussie born made him one step closer to being with him. Tomas was growing on him by the second. He'd never felt so much for someone so fast, and it was dizzying. And exhilarating.

"My grandfather died. Papa took over the family business. What about you?"

"Wollongong, born and bred. Came out here a couple of years ago to get into the big movies and fell into the other kind instead."

"How'd you do that?" Tomas was warming to the Aussie man beside him. They had something in common and could maybe be friends.

Roger shrugged and gave a small laugh. "Still not sure. I was auditioning for big movies, little independents as you do, and met Marcus. He asked if I had a problem getting my gear off. I said no. I built up to the gay porn. At first, I was an extra, and then had the starring role in straight movies. When Marcus found out I was gay, he asked if I'd be interested in switching. I gave it a go and liked it."

"How do you…?" Tomas blushed and glanced away.

"I like a man who blushes," Roger teased.

The red glow deepened. "How do you not get involved when you're doing it?"

"You block yourself off. You're just an actor in a movie seducing your partner."

"Is it hard?"

"Well…I always am."

"Oh." Tomas briefly closed his eyes.

"Why don't you come and watch. It's not so bad."

"It's a steam room. It will be."

Roger laughed and slapped him on the back again.

"Come on."

They made it back to the stage as the actors took their places.

Roger attended to his light, and Tomas walked over to stand beside Violet and Bette.

"All right, everyone, places," Marcus yelled as he barged over to his chair. "In five, four, three, two, one, and…action."

During the movie, Roger occasionally glanced over at Tomas. Most of the time he was looking at the ground, but when he wasn't, there was unadulterated pleasure on his face. The memories of that time were obviously coming back in a rush over and over, but then he'd look ashamed and glance away before looking back and remembering.

He's sweet, Roger thought. *Still young, unaffected. Gorgeous, beautiful, young, sweet.* He found himself smiling as the movie action rolled to a stop.

"And cut," Marcus yelled. "Print, we're done. See you all Monday." He noticed Violet with Bette and a hot young stud. "And who do we have here?" He stalked over to them. "Bette, Violet, and who are you?" He eyed Tomas up and down. "Fresh meat?"

Tomas frowned, clearly uncomfortable with the attention. "Definitely not!"

"And why not?" Marcus bellowed. "You're gorgeous. Look at you. Strong, athletic, dark and exotic. What are you…Italian?"

"Half Greek," Tomas replied quietly.

"How do you be half Greek?" Marcus inquired.

Tomas took a step back at the attention. "I'm also

half Australian."

"Australia." The light dawned. "Hey, Dencott, get over here." He waited while Roger walked over. "Aren't you Australian?"

"I am." Roger raised a mischievous brow at Tomas, making him blush.

"You know hot stuff here is half Australian." Marcus waved a cigar at Tomas.

Roger smiled at a blushing Tomas. "So I've heard."

"Well, what are the odds of that?" Marcus asked, puffing on his cigar. "Two Aussies in one movie."

"Oh, no, I don't," Tomas protested.

"Nonsense," Marcus bellowed. "An Aussie twosome."

"No, really, I—" Tomas cut in.

"Marcus," Roger spoke firmly. "Tomas isn't interested." He stared Marcus down. "Leave him alone and stop badgering him."

Marcus's gaze moved from Roger to Tomas and back to Roger. "Okay," he finally said. "I'll back off." He looked at the half Greek stud. "But I'm keeping my eye on you kid. I want you for my movies, and I'm gonna have you."

"Back off, Marcus." Roger laid a hand on his arm. "It's time we all got going home. Ladies, why don't I walk you to your cars?" He held an arm out for Bette and Violet and escorted them and Tomas out to their cars. "Pushy isn't he," he muttered to Tomas.

"Ah, yeah," Tomas replied. "Very." He opened the car door.

"Hey, um, what are you doing this weekend?" Roger asked.

Butterflies fluttered around Tomas's stomach. "Ah, nothing, at this stage."

Roger shrugged. "How about hanging out? I can show you the sights, introduce you to some friends. Show you some of the places that are safe to hang out."

"Ah." Tomas breathed and backed up to the car. "I don't…"

"He'd love to," Bette called through the door. "Come to my place tomorrow. 2715 Orchid Way, Coral Gables. About ten."

"Uh, Bette," Tomas muttered.

"Oh, for heaven's sake, you need to make friends, so deal with it. Now say goodbye and get in."

Tomas blushed, embarrassed by the motherly tone. "Ah, bye." He slid into the car.

Roger smiled. "Bye."

*****

Promptly, at ten the next morning, Roger turned up in shorts and a tank. It was a hundred out, and he was already hot. Not because of the weather, but because he was spending the day with Tomas Stephanopoulos.

The door opened, and there he stood dressed in the same outfit; shorts and a tank. All tanned, toned and terrific.

"Hey." Roger felt his heart swell along with a few other things.

"Hey, uh, just give me a minute." Tomas popped back inside, and Roger turned to look at the front garden, lush and green and buzzing with God's creatures. *Breathe Roger, breathe.*

"Hey, I'm ready." Tomas closed the door behind him and saw the Mustang convertible. "Cool ride. You got sunscreen?"

"Yeah, in the glove box."

Tomas grinned. "Still call it a glove box?" He jumped into the passenger side. "Cool."

"Of course." Roger got in beside him. "I've only been here two years; it's still bonnet, boot, and glove box. But getting used to Fahrenheit instead of Celsius and driving on the other side of the car *and* road, that's just plain weird."

Tomas laughed, and Roger gunned the engine and drove out of the driveway both so lost in each other they didn't even notice the car tailing them.

"So, where are you taking me?" Tomas asked as the warm Miami breeze whipped his black locks back and forth.

"I thought I'd take you to the beach. Have you checked that out yet?"

"Not yet."

"We could have lunch at a little place owned by a friend of mine, and one that is very gay-friendly. You won't be harassed there. We can spend the afternoon strolling Miami Beach, then I can drop you off to freshen up, and I'll take you to *Love Stick.* It's fast becoming the place to be here in Miami."

"Sounds great. I haven't been out much since we got here. I've spent weeks training the ladies, and haven't had much time for anything else."

"I think it will help if you have a fellow Aussie

show you around and we can talk about home if you want to."

"God, I miss the place sometimes. My grandparents were out a couple of months ago. Papa brings them over for mama so she still gets to see them."

"That's nice of him." Roger took a right-hand turn.

"Yeah, means a lot to us too."

"How many of you are there?"

"Just me and my two brothers. I'm the middle child."

"Ah." Roger grinned. "The dastardly middle child."

"The quiet, non-boisterous middle child."

"Ah, well, that explains everything."

"What do you mean by that?"

"Your whole demeanour is quiet, reserved, introverted." Roger pulled to a stop at Miami Beach.

"Yeah," Tomas said. "I guess I am."

"So, what do you think?" Roger sat up on the back of his seat. "Is our beach as good as Mykonos or Australia?"

Tomas joined him and took in the sweeping beach with its glorious yellow sand and aqua blue water. "It's great," he said enthusiastically. "Not as good as Mykonos mind you, but still great."

After a fun-filled day that made Tomas relax, Roger dropped him off to change and picked him up an hour later. They spent a couple of hours at *Love Stick*, the restaurant bar that was the current popular spot for gay men. Roger introduced Tomas to some of his friends, and they relaxed over drinks and music. Arriving at Bette's just after one in the morning, Roger escorted Tomas to the front door.

"What are you doing?" Tomas smiled.

"Escorting my date to the front door," Roger replied.

Tomas stopped short. "Date?"

"Well…isn't that what we've been on?" Roger arched a brow.

Tomas's mouth moved, but nothing came out.

"Is being on a date too much for you right now?" Roger asked softly.

"Yes," came out in a rush. The feelings welled in Tomas's throat.

Roger nodded. "Understandable. Just two guys hanging out then. I'll go and leave you to it." He held out his hand. "Good night."

Confused, Tomas took the hand offered. "Night." And held on.

So did Roger.

Tomas blinked and breathed.

So did Roger.

Tomas breathed and reluctantly let go. "Night."

So did Roger. "Night."

From the shadows in the street, Luiz watched the scene play out on the terrace. The anger boiled over and burned his insides. His fists clenched either side of him. *No one touches my Tomas but me. No one. I have no idea who you are or what you want, but it won't be my Tomas.*

*****

Monday morning at eight, Tomas had a one on one

with Marie Von Burstenstore. She had been with Violet and Bertha at *The Joy Stick.*

"And go down on your right leg, extend your left leg back, arms up above your head." Tomas held his left hand on her stomach as he slid his right hand down the back of her left leg. "Extend it, straighten the hips." He shifted her hips slightly. "Lengthen the spine, reach back." His hands slid up her spine to her head. "And stretch."

"Oh," she groaned. "That's good."

"Stretching always feels good." Tomas slid his hand down her back, over her hips and down her leg. "Stretch it out."

"Oh." She sighed. "I meant you. You're good."

"So I've been told. Now come back up and do the same to the other side." He stood as she did and walked around her while she positioned herself to stretch.

"Are you gay, Tomas?" Marie slid down, right leg back, left leg steady.

"What's that got to do with anything?" He slid his hand down her leg to strengthen it.

"I want a man. I *need* a man. A healthy, fit, young man. And I'd love it to be you, but if you're gay, then that's obviously not going to happen." She turned her head. "Unless you change your mind or decide you're Bi or something. I need a man, Tomas."

"I'm not that man, Marie." He smiled. "Do the child yoga pose for a few moments, and we're done for the morning."

"Maybe I should have snagged that Luiz stud from

Bertha. He was hot." Her voice was muffled as her head was on the floor, but he still heard her.

"What about Luiz?" His heart pounded like a hundred horses' hooves in his chest.

"Did you ever meet him? I think she took him to the Greek Islands with her. Young, hot, a Mediterranean style delicacy. Now that's she's dropped him I wonder if he's free." She slowly sat up, knowing full well Tomas had met Luiz, having heard it all from Bertha at the club. She just wanted to see what Tomas said about it. "She hasn't said what happened. Did you meet him?"

"Uh." Tomas walked over to the side table for a towel. "Briefly." He handed it to her as she stood.

"Hot hunk of horny looking man meat, isn't he." She dabbed her face while watching his. "I'd love to get that into me. What about you?"

Tomas blushed and stayed in control. "I'll see you tomorrow, Marie."

*****

During the week, Tomas was bombarded with personal invitations into the ladies' boudoirs which he politely turned down. Now, with it being Friday night, he wanted some male company.

"Why don't you call him?" Bette checked herself in the hallway mirror. She was going out with the girls and had invited Tomas to come along, but he had declined.

"Call who?" he asked innocently, leaning against

the wall next to the mirror.

"Oh, pish," she scoffed. "You know full well who I mean. That young man from the studio. What's his name? Roger?"

"Yeah." Tomas drifted away. "Roger."

"From the look on your face, I'd say you were taken with him, so I suggest you call him. Right," she checked her purse, "I have my money, my powder, my lipstick. I'm off. Have fun and call him," she said as the door closed behind her.

Tomas wandered down the hallway to the French doors that led out to the back terrace, thinking about Roger. He wasn't sure if he should call. What if he was too busy? What if Roger wasn't interested? Was *he* interested? After what happened with Luiz he didn't want to rush into another relationship. Not that this was a relationship, just a summer thing, a friendship even. But still, the guilt lingered. He glanced down the hallway at the phone, wondering if he should call.

The phone rang.

Tomas bolted down the hall and picked it up. "Hello, Bette Olander's residence."

"Tomas? Is that you?"

"Roger?"

"Yeah, hi."

"Hi."

"I, uh, was wondering if you were doing anything tonight. It's been a hectic week, and I thought you might want to get together and do something."

"Uh, yeah, sure, but ah, I don't really feel like going out…maybe you could come over here…have dinner…" He waited while his insides freaked out.

"Sure. I'd love to. See you soon."

The dial tone sounded, and Tomas almost screamed for joy. *Calm down, calm, down.* He dropped the phone into the cradle and went in search of food in the kitchen. He found plenty in the well-stocked fridge.

"Do you need something, sir?" Webster asked, walking through the door.

"No, thanks, Webster. I'm having a guest over, but we'll make something ourselves. You have the night off."

Webster nodded. "Very well, sir."

Fifteen minutes later the doorbell rang, and Tomas ran like an eager puppy to answer it. *Calm down, calm down.* He checked himself in the mirror before opening the door. He saw Roger's smiling face and his stomach did flip flops. "Hi, come in."

"Hey," Roger said. "Busy week?" He stepped into the entrance. "Wow, as impressive as the outside." Between the wide hall, sweeping staircase, chandeliers at ten paces and all of the ornate woodwork, it really was quite impressive.

"You hungry?" Tomas shut the door.

"Ah, yeah." *But not for food,* Roger thought.

"Great. The butler's got the night off, so I thought we'd make something." He led the way into the kitchen that was opposite the ballroom at the back of the house. "I can cook a few things, but I'm not great." He pulled open the fridge door. "See anything you like?"

"Absolutely."

"Great. We can—" Tomas's hand was grabbed,

making him stop. He looked into Roger's eyes, so brown that he drowned in them. His heart pounded, and so did the blood causing his penis to become engorged. His breath was hard.

"Can I kiss you?" Roger asked softly. "I've wanted to all week."

Tomas swallowed the lump that had risen to his throat. "Ah…I…" He breathed out. "Yes…" came out in a whisper.

The fridge door forgotten, Roger stepped toward him. He was six three and towered over Tomas by four inches. He moved slowly, not wanting to scare him. His fingers interweaved with Tomas's and everything about his being was on fire. It had been a long time since he'd been with anyone as no one had interested him. But now this beautiful half Greek God was standing before him. His lips moved in and landed on their chosen spot.

It was sweet, gentle, but Tomas wanted more. He kissed back, opening his lips and delving his tongue into Roger's mouth. *Oh, God, he feels so good. It feels so right. Roger feels so right.* His arms slid around Roger's waist as their tongues danced wildly in a synchronised tribal beat. "Oh, God," he gasped in between tongue mating. "I want you. I want this."

Hands slid all over the place, exploring, touching, caressing. Mouths and tongues tasted until Roger finally pulled away and took Tomas's face in his hand. "Is this what you want? You've only been with one person. You're still new to this."

"Yes," Tomas whispered. "Yes." After a kiss, he led

Roger upstairs to his room. He had the opposite side of the house to Bette, so it wouldn't disturb her to have a guest over. He locked the door before walking over to the bed and flinging back the covers. He turned to Roger.

"I want you," he whispered and slid his hands under Roger's polo top, moving them up his body to push the top over his head. Greedy hands slid down, up, all around. "Oh, God look at you," he gasped softly. Hands slid into shorts and briefs and slid them down to set Roger's erect manhood free. With trembling hands, Tomas stroked him. He hardened further, so he massaged him.

A groan escaped from Roger's throat before he grasped Tomas's hands. Undressing him, he marvelled at the tanned Adonis. Dark hair spattered his body in all the right places, especially around his twelve inch cock. "Jesus, Tomas." His hand slid over the package. "That's a hell of a cock you've got."

"Take it," Tomas whispered. "It's yours. Do what you want with it."

Roger's thumbs slid down over the tip getting a sharp gasp, and a head tilt in reaction. He motioned for Tomas to lie on the bed and proceeded to do exactly what he wanted. Burying his head in Tomas's crotch, he took great delight in feeding from the fountain.

Hours after, they slowed down, languishing on piles of pillows as the night-time summer breeze wafted through the open balcony doors.

"Jesus, Tomas." Roger's fingers trailed up and down his abdomen. "And you reckon you've been with only one man and had one experience. That's a hell of a lot of experience for one encounter."

Tomas kissed Roger's chest as he lay curled against it. "It was an encounter, but being with you made it all better. It's relaxing. No concerns, no worries. I'm still learning, and you're a great teacher." His fingers slid around Roger's torso. "You can teach me so much."

"You're definitely open to it. That's for sure." Roger smirked. "Very open."

Tomas slid a leg over Roger's. "Absolutely. I want you to teach me everything you know."

"And what about what you'll teach me?" Roger gently slid a finger across Tomas's face. "What will you teach me, Tomas Stephanopoulos? How to be young again?"

"Aren't you?" Tomas smiled "You can't be much older than me."

"I'm twenty-nine, nearly thirty."

"Well, that's okay." Tomas kissed him. "Means you have more experience at this. More time to learn things, do things." Another kiss, long and lingering. Followed by another and another as Tomas made his way down Roger's smooth bronzed body to the inner sanctum. Tomas had never taken a man before so set about things slowly. He gently kissed Roger's cock all the way along the shaft, making it rise to the occasion. Planting kisses all over it, he gently kissed the end, getting a sharp intake of breath in return. Slowly, gently, he licked and tasted before sliding his mouth over the top.

"Ah!" Roger arched. "Make sure to relax your

mouth, no teeth," he gasped, spreading his legs for Tomas to lie between.

Tomas positioned himself and took Roger whole, regaling him with his tongue before sliding off and turning around. He sat with his back to Roger and mounted him as Roger's hands went to his hips to guide him.

"Ah," Tomas groaned, grinding up and down. "Ah, God." He rubbed himself until they both came and he dismounted. Turning around he slid up Roger's body and lay half on half off as Roger enveloped him in his arms.

"You're learning." Roger kissed his forehead. "Definitely learning."

In the shadows on the street, Luiz clicked the light on his watch. Five past two. He eyed the Mustang in the driveway and knew it belonged to that guy he'd seen with Tomas last week. He'd been there since after seven and hadn't left. He glanced around to make sure no one was watching and proceeded to race up the driveway to the car, remove his knife from his pocket, and stab all four tyres. He unscrewed the petrol cap and poured sugar into the tank, then scratched up and down and along the sides, trunk and hood. When he was satisfied, he raced back to the street, and with a smirk slipped into the shadows and disappeared.

They woke in each other's arms, floating out of a deep, peaceful sleep to find themselves enmeshed. It was as if they'd been doing it all of their lives. The warm breeze drifted through the curtains and over their semi-naked bodies. The sheet was a tangled mess and wrapped around their legs.

Roger breathed deeply. His arms were around Tomas as though it was the most natural thing in the world, as was waking together. This was something he wanted to do every single day. He'd never met anyone like him, and for all the partners he'd had, none were like Tomas. Maybe it was his naivety, his newness, his lack of experience with sex in general, let alone gay sex. He stroked his lover's chiselled cheek bone and marvelled at the man beside him and the way he fitted him like a glove, as though they were made for each other.

Tomas breathed in and opened his eyes a fraction. He was in Roger's arms, and it felt like heaven, felt so right. His head was on his chest, and he smiled, sliding his hand up Roger's side. He tilted his head back to look at his lover who was watching back. He blushed and buried his head in Roger's chest. "Morning."

Roger kissed his head. "Morning. How do you feel?"

Tomas smiled. "Happy, alive, free." He moved upward, and Roger rolled onto his side so they were facing each other. Stroking Roger's face, he said, "I'm so happy."

Roger matched his smile with one of his own. "Good." Their fingers entwined between them. "So, what do you want to do today?"

"You." Tomas grinned and kissed him. "All day."

*****

Sunday afternoon, they rolled out of bed and had a late lunch on the back terrace.

"What are you doing this week?" Tomas asked around a strawberry. He bit into the sweet delight. "Anything interesting?"

"I'm filming a couple of movies and helping out on others." Roger took a sip of freshly squeezed juice. "Wanna come watch?"

Tomas's mood blackened. He'd forgotten that Roger was a porn star and now the thought of his man having sex with someone else disgusted him.

Roger noticed the change. "It's just work. Just a job, nothing more. I made the decision a long time ago to never get involved with people I worked with. So I never have. And many of my co-stars also have partners, so there's no involvement. We get in, get out, job done."

Tomas glanced up. "What's it like?"

"What?"

"Having sex with someone in front of people, in front of cameras, people watching you naked and," he made hand gestures, "being connected physically."

Roger set down his glass. "At first it was weird. When I did the two straight porn movies, it was weird on two levels. One, because everyone was watching, and two, because I didn't want to be with women. When I moved to gay porn, it was a bit easier being with another man, and I got used to having Marcus yell out directions. He doesn't always, but sometimes, you just have to forget they're all there. Shut them out and get on with it."

"Have you…" Tomas played with his napkin. "Ever had a partner that disagreed with what you do?"

"No."

Tomas looked into Roger's big brown eyes. "Ever?"

"I've been single the whole time I've been in America, so you're the first. Do you disagree with what I do?"

"I…" Tomas shook his head and shrugged. "I don't know. All of this is new to me and still a bit weird. And I'm uncomfortable with being on display."

"You're not. Unless you want to be," Roger said slyly.

"What do you mean?"

"Well…" Roger raised a brow. "What if *we* did a movie together?"

Tomas blinked. "Us? In a porn movie?"

Roger blinked. "Yes."

Tomas looked everywhere but at Roger. "I…ah… I… Oh, God."

"Would it be so wrong? You, me, you could make a lot of money doing it."

"Money's not the issue."

"Why don't you come and watch me do a movie and see how you feel?"

"Watch you?" Tomas was horrified. He didn't need to see his new lover having sex with anyone else.

"Tomas," Roger said. "It's not that bad. I'd love to do one with you. Why don't you come by tomorrow night and watch?"

Tomas sighed in defeat. "Maybe."

"Meantime." Roger wiped his mouth. "I better get going. Walk me to my car?" His fingers reached for Tomas's and wound around them. They walked out to his car and stopped in horror. "What…the…fuck…"

"Oh, my God, Roger." Tomas stared, horrified at the damage to the Mustang. The paint had been scratched; the tyres were all flat.

"What the fuck," Roger repeated, circling the car to check the damage. "It's scratched on every surface. Fucking hell!"

"How could this have happened?" Tomas asked, standing on the mansion steps.

"Fucked if I know." Roger ran a hand through his hair. "But it's going to cost me a fucking bundle."

"So, what do we do? Call a garage?" Tomas asked.

"Guess I'm gonna have to. You got a phone book?"

Half an hour later, the tow truck arrived and hitched the Mustang up, towing it away to be repaired. Tomas drove Roger to the auto shop and sixty minutes later found it was worse than they'd first thought. Sugar had also been poured into the gas tank.

"Fuck it!" Roger spat, pacing around the office. "Who the fuck would do this? And at Bette's place. That means someone *came onto* the property and trashed my car in the middle of the night. That's fucked up that is."

Tomas tried to soothe him. "Maybe it was the local hooligans. I don't know. But maybe you should make a police report."

"Oh, hell yeah, I'm making a police report." Roger stood with his hands on his hips. "As soon as I can get another car."

"Is there a rental place around? I'll drive you," Tomas told him.

*****

Eight o'clock Monday night, Tomas reluctantly popped by *Seralift* studios and stood in the background as Roger filmed his love scene with a tall, dark African American man, and regardless of the reservations he'd had, he actually found it quite arousing. He watched the way Roger expertly manipulated the man into doing what he wanted. The way he moved him, bent him, made him do everything right from the beginning. From the kisses to the touches to the thrusting in perfect sync.

Tomas found himself in need of relief; relief he would find only in Roger. For all his doubts, what he'd just witnessed was a hell of a turn on. When it was over, the crew dispersed and only Roger was left.

"So…what did you think?" Roger slipped on a robe.

"Of what?" Tomas smiled coyly.

"Of the movie. What I do." Roger stood in front of him and took his hands. "What did you think?"

Tomas linked his fingers through Roger's. "Ah…" He blushed.

"Yes," Roger quietly cajoled.

Tomas blushed harder. "It was…hot…"

"Good." Roger pulled him into his arms and kissed him. "Would you like to try it out?"

"Try what out?" Tomas stroked Roger's chest.

"Making a movie together," Roger said against his lips.

"Ah." Tomas pulled back. "I know it looked hot, but…"

"Let's give it a go." Roger's fingers slid under Tomas's top and down his shorts. "I can go again. We can film it, and you could be a star, Tomas Stephanopoulos," Roger whispered against his cheek. His fingers circled Tomas's manhood. "You could be a star, Tomas."

Tomas groaned and leant in, resting his head on Roger's cheek. "Oh, God." The pressure from Roger's hand was doing damage to his resolve. The manipulating fingers added to the destruction. "It couldn't hurt to try it. Just once." He touched his lips to Roger's.

Roger grinned. "Let's make a movie." He led Tomas to the steam room set.

"Oh, no, I can't." Tomas baulked.

"No," Roger said. "Time to make new memories so you can get rid of the old ones." He set the video cameras rolling, turned on the lights and the steam machine. "Now, let's make some magic." He dropped his robe and helped Tomas out of his clothes before taking him into the steam room. His fingers slid up Tomas's arm, and he leant in close. He pleasured and pleased and aroused him in all manners using his mouth and tongue, and had Tomas shaking at the knees, weak from the attack on his senses. Weak from the steam.

"Oh," Tomas whispered. "Oh, God," escaped into the steam as Roger went down on him. "Oh, God." He held him in place, pulsating in time to the rhythm of his mouth. "Oh, God."

Roger's tongue lapped it up and kept on going, up Tomas's torso and into his mouth. He rubbed his erection against his lover's and turned him around to face the wall, spreading his legs with his knee.

Tomas looked weakly over his shoulder. "I want you."

Roger kissed him and stood between his legs hard and full and ready for take-off. He rubbed himself back and forth, pushing against the back of Tomas's testicles, pushing up toward the anus. Back and forth he rubbed while his hand slid around to the front to do equal damage. He handled, cajoled, kneaded.

"Oh, God," Tomas cried against the wall, his head falling back. "Oh, God." He came in Roger's hands, and Roger entered, bringing him to the brink again. "Oh, God," Tomas yelled. "Oh, God, oh, God, oh, God." He came a second time and collapsed against the wall. "Oh, God, what you do to me."

"And I want to do it every single minute of every single day." Roger kissed his neck and nuzzled his ear.

Tomas gasped, waiting for his breath to settle. "I want you to do it every single minute of every single day."

Roger's fingers enclosed Tomas's on the wall beside their faces. "I want to come inside of you, make love to you, make you mine."

"I want to be yours," Tomas panted. "I *am* yours. All yours."

Roger kissed his way along Tomas's shoulder, looking out into the studio. Marcus was standing there open-mouthed and staring, with Violet beside him, fanning herself with her handkerchief.

"We're done," Roger whispered and withdrew,

quickly collecting his robe and Tomas's clothes. He blocked the view so Tomas could dress. "We have company," he whispered when he was done. "Be cool."

Tomas panicked, but nodded, and let Roger lead him out of the set and over to Marcus and Violet. Having his love life on view was not what he wanted, and having sex with people watching was not on. His stomach tightened in knots.

"Enjoy the show?" Roger asked, keeping a protective step in front of Tomas. "It was a private moment between a couple… But what did you think?"

"Fucking brilliant," Marcus said. "That was the horniest, steamiest, best piece of fucking I've seen in my whole career in the industry. You two," he thrust a finger at them, "have the most explosive fuckable chemistry I've ever seen. You, my boy," he told Tomas, "are now my biggest star, and the two of you," he waved his finger, "are now going to be a couple if you're not already. But I mean in movies. Just the two of you, starring in my movies. They're going to be big, big I tell ya. Welcome to the industry kid. Come on, Violet, let's make some plans." He walked off leaving her standing there.

"Well!" She fluttered her hanky. "Now I know what all of us ladies are missing out on. Whoo, hot in here." She quickly followed her ex-husband.

Roger shut down the cameras and steam pump, leaving the overhead lights on. "I'll just get dressed, and we can go."

While he dressed, Tomas desperately thought through what had just happened. He was being intimate with his lover, but Marcus and Violet had been watching. Could he do that for a living? Could he do that and more in front of other people, a whole sound stage of crew, watching, filming it for the whole world to see?

He wrapped his arms around himself and held on tight. Could he do this in front of people for the world to see? Would being with Roger make it all worthwhile? He watched Roger do up his pants and marvelled at his body, knowing he was in love with the man before him. So desperately in love. For the first time ever. For the first time in his twenty-two years, he was in love. And it was with a man. Could he do it *for* him? Could he do it *with* him? His brow furrowed. He felt the pain of indecision and knew he had to make a choice. Work *with* his lover, or watch him work with other men. Could he do that? Could he seriously stand by while his new lover made love to other men for a living? In that very moment, he didn't know. But it was a decision he was going to have to make.

Once Roger was dressed, they left hand in hand.

In the shadows of the studio, Luiz lurked behind a sound stage. He'd followed Tomas there and watched the first movie, then stayed and watched, in horror, him replicate their time in the steam room at the resort.

"No one does that with my Tomas," he spat viciously. "No one touches him, fucks him, or sucks him the way I do, and that little cock sucker's going to pay for taking Tomas's memory of me. *No one* gets my man but me." He held up his large silver knife, and the light glinted off the cold hard metal.

Oh, no. No one gets my Tomas. Clearly, my first warning was not enough. No, looks like I'll have to step it up a notch.

Leaving the studio he hid in the shadows, watching them walk hand in hand to their car and leave.

No one gets my Tomas. He brandished the knife.

October 1977

Marcus raised his glass. "Cheers to a very important—"

"And lucrative," Violet butted in.

"And lucrative," Marcus continued, "business venture."

"Cheers."

Everyone was at Seralift Manor, the magnificent ten bedroom, ten bath mansion spread across a cove on the glorious Hollywood Beach. Bette, Bertha and Willow to Marie, Beatrice and all of the ladies that Tomas had been training for the last two months were there, plus their partners, husbands, and gigolos, and all of the stage crew at *Seralift Productions*. Not to mention the other talented actors in the movies plus their partners, and friends of Roger and Tomas. It was a huge affair for hundreds of people all decked out in their finery.

Roger and Tomas were resplendent in tuxedos with their arms around each other. Bette, Bertha and Willow were dressed up to the nines in sparkling jewels as were the other ladies. Champagne was flowing freely, and a band played the latest disco on the back terrace facing the water's edge. It was beyond anything Tomas had ever dreamt of going to.

Roger pulled him aside. "Can you believe it's been a month already?"

Tomas shook his head. "No, can you? I can't even believe…" He blushed.

"What?" Roger leant on a sideboard, pulling Tomas into his arms. "What?"

Tomas looked up into the big brown eyes and slid his arms around his neck. "I can't believe we have sex for a living." One month ago he'd made a choice; to make sex movies with his new lover. For all the inexperience, for all the naïvety, for all the things he didn't know and was yet to learn about love and relationships, he knew he wanted to be with Roger. And so he'd made the decision to be with him in movies as well as life.

Roger grinned. "Well, you did say you wanted to do it all day every day."

"Or in our case, all night. I don't want to give up my training unless I have to." Tomas kissed him lightly. "I love you, and I'm so glad I met you."

Roger pulled him tighter until their crotches pushed together. "I love you, too, and I am so glad you came into my life." They kissed, and it deepened.

"All right you two save it for the movies," Marcus bellowed, seeing them pull apart, blush, giggle, and then hug. "You were damn right, Violet. He *is* a talent."

She sighed and sipped her champagne. "Just a pity he's gay. All of my friends want to try him out."

"After watching the steamy fucking these two get up to, so do I." Marcus puffed on his cigar. "He is *one hell* of a boy, and they made *one hell* of a movie together."

"A lethal combination," Violet told Bette who was standing with them. "We're so glad you persuaded him to come here."

"He nearly didn't," Bette replied. "It was that stupid fling with Bertha's Luiz that nearly stuffed it all up. He had to take advantage of poor Tomas and make him feel guilty as hell. Thank God Bertha dumped him and got Tomas to forget about him. Otherwise..." She shrugged. "No Tomas."

They waiter behind them froze. Behind the bleached blond hair, coloured contact lenses, and black rimmed glasses, no one was going to recognise him. Luiz had managed to finagle his way in as a member of staff and had hovered close to Roger and Tomas without anyone noticing. As long as his tray was always full of champagne, no one cared.

He casually glanced at Tomas hugging Roger by the side doors. If Bertha hadn't dumped him, Tomas wouldn't be in Miami? It wasn't his fault the kid felt ten tonnes of guilt for fucking a man. It had been the most wondrous time of his life, spending hours in the sun inside Tomas making love in the heady rays and cool tropical breeze. The feel of Tomas's rod of pleasure against his was magnificent. He'd never met a man so young with so big a rod, and he'd had it inside *and* in his mouth. Oh, God, it was magnificent.

He hardened and quickly left the room. He needed to relieve himself and headed for the private bathroom for guests at the side of the house. He shut and locked the door, unzipped and pulled it out before turning around.

"Hey, it's full in here!" a man exclaimed before seeing the magnificent penis before him.

"I need relief," Luiz told him. "Now."

"Need a hand with that?" The man shook his off and left it hanging.

"If you don't mind." Luiz stepped towards him.

The man turned, bent over the sink, and Luiz entered, thrusting across the finish line to grunts and groans from the man. He shuddered. The man shuddered. Luiz stayed inside and pulled a small vial of white powder from his pants pocket. "Coke?"

The man grabbed the vial, spread some on his left hand and snorted it back. "Oh, God, that's good." He clenched his anal muscles. "Again?"

Luiz examined the man. Average height, long, dirty blond hair, green eyes, good-looking, and a member of Marcus Seralift's stable. "Only if you snort some more." Luiz reached around to squeeze the man's dick.

*****

Bertha sidled up to Bette with her new beau. "Don't they make a charming pair? I'm so glad Tomas found someone of his own."

"Someone who's not yours, you mean." Bette's eyes twinkled.

"I didn't mean that." Bertha grinned mischievously. "Not what I meant at all." She watched Tomas stroke

Roger's face as he gazed adoringly at him. "He really looks like he's in love."

"Yes, yes he does," Bette said. "Let's hope he finds some happiness after this fiasco with his brothers and Luiz."

"Speaking of his brothers..." Marcus came up to them. "You'll never guess what I've just found out. Tomas, Roger, get over here." He waved them over.

"What is it?" Bette asked. "You know his brothers?"

"Know?" Marcus laughed raucously. "Wait until you hear."

Roger and Tomas came up to them. "You bellowed," Roger said.

"Tomas, my boy, we've been making movies for four weeks now and have yet to come up with a name for you. Well, I found one. *Tomas Stefan.*"

Tomas frowned. "It's just a short version of my name. Nothing different."

"Exactly. *But*...it's also the name your brothers are using." He brandished two 8x10 photos, holding them so the blank backs were facing out and they couldn't see them yet. "Guess who have gotten themselves into the porn industry?"

The blood drained from Tomas's face. "No." His head moved slowly from left to right and back again.

"Oh, *yes*, my boy." With a flourish, he turned the photos around. "Say hello to Carlo and Pedro Stefan."

Tomas looked at the photos of his brothers, slowly reaching out to take them. "My God, Carlos... Pedro." He studied the promotional shots of the brothers he hadn't seen in months. Carlos in the pool, and Pedro with the city of New York in the background. "Where are they? *What* are they?"

"Carlos is in Hollywood with Harry DeVille, and Pedro in New York with Greta Von Burro. Two *very* big producers in their cities."

"Wow." Tomas shook his head in amazement. "I haven't seen Carlos since June when he disappeared, and Pedro since July. They look good. They look healthy and happy. And clearly not in jail."

"Jail?" Marcus asked.

"They fled Mykonos under shady circumstances, and the cops were after them." Tomas moved the photos closer to Roger. "My brothers."

"Good looking young men. Clearly hot genes run in the family." His hand slid over Tomas's ass. "Very hot genes."

Tomas's blush deepened. "Can I keep these?" he asked. "I don't have any pictures of my brothers."

"Sure, kid, sure. I got copies of their movies too. We'll have to watch them later."

"Are they gay porn as well?" Bette asked.

"No, straight, but fucking hot from the quick bit I saw."

"Carlos always was sticking it to the ladies," Tomas said. "I don't think there were many women left on Mykonos who hadn't had the pleasure of Carlos Stephanopoulos between their legs."

Marcus cocked a brow, and Violet stifled a giggle. "We'd better see that video, then," she said.

*****

The man in the bathroom finished snorting the contents of the vial. "Oh, that's good stuff. Got any more?"

Luiz zipped up his pants and produced another vial. "Snort away my friend, but make it quick. I gotta get back to work."

"Fuck snorting it," the man said and threw the powder into his mouth. "I'll just swallow it. Like I just swallowed you."

Luiz tucked in his shirt. "Yes, you did. And my, what a big mouth you have." He noticed the man change. Just a slight twitch of the face, a look in the eye. He smoothed back his hair. "Gotta go, enjoy." He unlocked and opened the door, sneaking a peek left and right. When he saw no one, he headed back to the kitchen.

*****

"Apparently, Harry and Greta both say they have the hottest star in the porn world. It's going to be the battle of the brothers, and now that we know, we'll be hot on their trail," Marcus told the group.

Murmurs and smashing glass erupted behind them, and they turned to see Jeff Fastwater stumbling into the room, pants unzipped, cock swinging from side to side.

The women gasped in delight; the men snickered at the size. The wait staff dropped their trays at the sight before them. Jeff stumbled, incoherent, wiping his nose and sniffing.

Marcus strode over to confront him. "Put that

piece of crap away before I cut it off. This is a respectable party."

Jeff simply sneered at him, sniffing and wiping his nose on his coat sleeve.

"Now," Marcus demanded.

His tone sent Jeff's cock back into his pants as he fumbled with his zip.

"You're clearly on something." Marcus noticed the red, watery eyes as security took an arm each and dragged Jeff away.

Jeff was clearly not in charge of his faculties let alone in possession of a set of balls to man up and keep his habits to himself at a party such as this.

Marcus watched the two guards drag a struggling Jeff to the door where he promptly fell to his knees before falling face first onto the floor. "Oh, for God's sake, get him up." Marcus bellowed.

The guards bent down. "Wait," one said, spying blood coming from Jeff's nose. He quickly checked for a pulse while everyone crowded into the large entrance way. The guard stood and turned to his boss. "He's dead."

Everyone gasped in shock.

"What?" Marcus asked.

"He has no pulse. He's dead," the guard repeated.

Everyone stared in shock.

"Call the police," Marcus bellowed. "Call an ambulance. See if you can help him." He stumbled over to the body, but the guard stopped him.

"No, sir, he's bleeding from the nose, don't touch him." He held Marcus back while the other guard ushered everyone back into the ballroom.

Ten minutes later the police and coroner's van arrived.

"So, what do we have here?" An average height man with salt and pepper curls and a beige trench coat came through the door bearing his badge. "Detective Barden, Miami PD. Who's the victim?"

"Jeff Fastwater," Marcus replied dejectedly. "He's an actor."

"And what are we all doing here tonight?" Barden continued, looking around at the old women and young men.

"Having a party," Violet replied and stepped forward. "Violet Seralift. This is my ex-husband's home, Marcus Seralift. We run a movie production studio, and Jeff is…*was*…one of our actors."

"And what kind of movies do you make?" Barden flipped open his notebook. At fifty-five he'd been hoping to retire soon, but a spate of deaths had kept him working, so it wasn't the first time he'd seen a young person with white powder around their nose flat dead on the floor.

"Adult movies," she said calmly.

Barden blinked and kept his expression neutral. "You mean pornos?"

Violet blinked back. "If that's what you want to call them."

The coroner covered Jeff's body with a white sheet and called Barden over to the side of the room. "Probably an overdose. Too much snorting can cause bleeding, but I'll do an autopsy just to make sure."

"Thanks, Doc." Barden slapped him on the back

and walked over to Marcus who sat forlornly in a chair at the side of the hall. "Mr Seralift, can you tell me what happened?"

Marcus looked up, his eyes distant. "What?"

"Can you tell me what happened?"

"Clearly my ex is in a state of shock right now so I can tell you." Violet appeared at his side. "We were having a party when Jeff stumbled into the room with his pants unzipped. He was sniffing and wiping his nose and was very unstable on his feet. Marcus ordered security to throw him out, but when they reached the door, he fell to his knees and collapsed. We called you."

An officer came rushing through the doorway. "Detective, this fell out of the man's pocket when he was put into the van." He handed over a photograph.

Barden took it and looked at it closely. It was of two men on a sound stage, smiling and laughing. And naked. "Mrs Seralift, do you recognise these two?" He showed her the photo.

"Why, yes, that's our sound stage. That's Roger and Tomas."

"And when would this have been taken?"

"Well, that looks like *Big Cock in Little China*; we only filmed that last week."

"And those two men are *where*, now?"

"Here."

"At the party?"

"Yes, in the ballroom." She pointed.

"How appropriate," Barden quipped. "Can you get them for me?"

"Of course." She hurried into the room and

returned with the two boys. "This is Roger Dencott and Tomas Stephanopoulos."

"Detective Barden," he introduced himself. "Stephanopoulos… What's that?"

"Greek," Tomas told him.

"Huh! Either of you boys know why this," he glanced at his notes, "Jeff Fastwater would have this in his pocket?" He handed the photo to them.

Roger took it, and they looked at it. "Is that from the movie last week?"

"Looks like it," Tomas said. "Why would he have a photo of it?"

"That's what *I'm* asking," Barden said. "Who was he to both of you?"

Roger shrugged. "Just a co-worker."

"In what sense?" Barden asked.

Roger cocked a brow. "He was in other movies, but we were co-workers."

"Mmm, mmm," Barden mumbled. "What about you, Stephanpopodopolous?"

"Stephanopoulos," Tomas corrected. "I think I only met Jeff last week. He'd been on holiday when I started, and then worked during the day while I worked at night. It was only briefly. In fact, I think it was on the set of that movie." He pointed to the photo in Roger's hand.

"Interesting," Barden murmured, making notes.

"Why?" Roger asked.

"Mmm? No reason. I'll take that photo and get on with it." He retrieved the photo and nodded at Violet. "Mrs Seralift. Mr Seralift." He looked at Marcus. "You going to be all right, Mr Seralift? I'll contact you during the week with details of the investigation."

Marcus raised his head. "What?"

"I'll let you know what's happening during the week, Mr Seralift." Barden left him sitting in a daze.

Luiz had been watching all of it from the background, quietly serving drinks and keeping an eye on Tomas and Roger. He'd slipped that photo into Jeff's pocket while he was snorting, so he hadn't noticed a thing. He waited to see what they would do and saw the confused expressions.

He wanted to run to his Tomas and take him into his arms. Tell him everything was going to be all right if he just came back to him. But he couldn't. Such a shame. He watched them walk back into the ballroom.

"How well did you know Jeff?" Tomas asked Roger. "Would he do something like this?"

"Like what? Collapse at a party?" Roger escorted him to the far side of the room.

Tomas shrugged. "Stumble around with his cock out and then fall down dead from a potential overdose."

"Well, I think that's something you can only do once and not over and over again." Roger grinned.

"Ladies and gentlemen," Violet called a few minutes later. "May I have your attention? Due to the unfortunate circumstances that have occurred, I need to bid you good night and please have a safe journey home. This party is at an end. Please gather your coats and head home. Good night." She left to escort Marcus upstairs.

Bette and Bertha wandered over to Roger and

Tomas. "It's sad that young people feel the need to take so many drugs that they lose their life."

"Yes," Bertha agreed. "I'm just glad we're over that."

"But what could have made him overdose at a party?" Bette asked.

"That's what we were just saying," Tomas said.

"And where did he get the drugs? Did he come with them and then take too much?" Bertha sipped on her champagne.

"I don't know. But I think we'd better go," Roger said, seeing the room empty out.

They all agreed and bade each other good night as they collected coats and wandered off to their cars. Tomas had moved in with Roger only two days previously, so on the way home they discussed it some more.

"I wonder if this has anything to do with my car being trashed in August." Roger turned the corner. "I've also noticed that some people have had stuff go missing at the studio. My car, stuff being stolen, now a death. I wonder of it's all connected?"

"Why would it be?" Tomas asked as they pulled into the underground car park. He got out and shut the door. "Stuff goes missing, stuff gets stolen, your car was appalling because it was on private property, and as for Jeff, as we all know, people do drugs and die because of them."

They walked upstairs, and Roger unlocked the door to his second floor apartment. It had beach views, was fully furnished, and was ten minutes from the local shops. "My car was personal," he said, pulling at his bow tie. "No one would randomly walk onto someone's property and trash a car. That was a personal attack, but for the life of me I have no idea who'd want to do that."

Tomas removed his coat and stepped out of his pants. "Well, I don't know, but I didn't know Jeff did drugs, so maybe we should all get together and make a list of everything that's happened."

"Maybe someone's out to get everyone working for Marcus? There's probably some porn kingpin who wants to take over and put him out of business." Roger helped Tomas out of his shirt and shorts. "And I know one kingpin who wants to take over *you*."

"Except you're still overdressed." Tomas pushed him away and pulled back the covers. "You need to—"

"Done."

Tomas looked over his shoulder. Roger was completely naked and standing to attention. "Perve!" he teased as Roger jumped him.

Luiz slowly walked up the stairs. He kept an eye out for other people and made his way to the apartment on the second floor. Pulling out the master key he'd had made, he opened the door and quietly closed it behind him. Hearing noises coming from the bedroom, he walked over to the door and saw them going at it like rabid dogs. He levelled his camera and clicked a few rounds.

"Mmm, mmm, what was that?" Tomas mumbled. He heard the clicking again. "Wait, Roger, what is that? Roger." He looked over Roger's shoulder and saw the outline of a man holding something in front of his face. "Roger, someone's here, someone's in the apartment. Oh, my God."

Roger's head spun around to see a shadowy figure move. "Hey." He flew out of bed, grabbed his robe and heard the front door slam. Flinging it open he looked out, but only heard heavy steps thudding down the stairs. Racing after them, he came to a stop in the car park before speeding from car to car. He saw no one before going back upstairs.

"Well?" Tomas locked the door behind him.

"I didn't catch anyone. He got away." Roger grabbed a drink from the fridge.

"How the hell did he get in?" Tomas hung the chain up and realised. "Did you put the chain on when we got home?"

Roger thought back. "Nope, just the lock."

"That's how then. We'd better make sure to chain it in future. We don't want to be broken into again. He was watching us, taking pictures of us making love. How many times has he been here? Has anyone else broken in? Has anyone else been following us into our home or taking pictures of us? Oh, my God." The lump rose in Tomas's throat, and he sat on the couch and wrapped his arms around himself. "How many times has he been here?"

"I don't know, but please don't panic." Roger sat beside him and rubbed his back. "Don't panic. Stay calm. You've locked and bolted the door. There's no one here now. It's okay. Stay calm." The softness of Tomas's bare skin aroused him, and his hand drifted up and down. "Let's go back to bed," he said softly. "I want you."

Tomas looked up into passion filled eyes, felt himself rise, and took Roger there on the couch.

*****

Luiz pulled the photo out of the rinse tray and hung it up. Developing the roll of film was easy in his hotel room, he'd done it for a few weeks now. He looked at them one by one. Tomas on the set with Roger, Roger with other men, Tomas being taken from behind, the other man's head cut off on purpose, Tomas with other men. It was a plan, and that plan was in phase three.

Phase one had been to trash Roger's car. Phase two was to take photos on set and steal stuff, and now phase three had gone off with a bang.

The beginning of the end.

He left the photos to dry and walked into the bedroom. Several boxes lay on the bed, each containing photos and vials of D-grade cocaine. So lethal it would kill you if you had too much as poor Mr Fastwater had found out.

Yes, Jeff Fastwater fucked hard and snorted harder. His two loves were men and cocaine. One addiction led to the other and Luiz had played upon that. Jeff couldn't resist cock and took whatever was offered, especially if coke came with it. And it didn't take much to find out. Just a quick search through Jeff's locker at the studio and a search of his apartment showed pictures of young men doing what he wanted them to do. Sucking his cock and snorting his drugs.

Phew! Luiz thought. *One down, so many to go. So*

many cock sucking perves that deserved to be taken out. And if it means splitting up Tomas and Roger so Tomas will be mine again, then Roger will just be collateral damage.

*****

Tomas arrived at the studios three days later to find the grounds covered in cop cars and trench-coated detectives. "What's going on?" he asked Roger as he met him at the door. "What's happened?"

"Brock Hardwood is dead." Roger watched the procession of cops moving back and forth like worker ants.

"Oh, my God, what? What do you mean, dead?" Tomas spied Detective Barden talking to Marcus. "What happened? How did he die? Who found him?"

"Don't know, don't know, I did." Roger shoved his hands into his jeans pockets.

Tomas stared at him. "*You* found him?"

Roger's eyes glazed over and he winced. "Yeah."

"Oh, my God."

"Oh, my God, indeed. Mr Dencott, I want a word with you." Barden walked over to them dressed in his usual grey suit and beige trench coat. "I want to know exactly what happened from start to finish. Don't leave anything out." He flipped open his pad. "Go."

Roger sighed. "We were on a break. I was chatting to some of the crew as I'd helped out with the stages earlier."

"You're a member of the crew as well?" Barden

interrupted.

"Yes. I help out with lighting, carting equipment, moving stages."

"Ah, multipurpose actor. Move on." Barden waved his pen at him.

"And when it was time to get the next set ready, I went ahead a few minutes earlier and found Brock on the floor. I rushed over, thinking he'd tripped and hurt himself, but…"

"But?"

Roger kicked his lips. "He was cold. So I checked for a pulse and found none." He shifted uncomfortably.

"When was the last time you saw Mr Hardwood?"

"After lunch when we were doing a movie."

"And what were you both *doing* in the movie?"

"He was acting in it, I was stage designer."

"So, a lot of *hands-on* experience?"

Roger eyed the man before him. He came up to Roger's shoulder. "What are you implying, Detective?"

Barden cocked a lip. "Well, you're all gay here, aren't you? Working on movies where you're all having sex with each other, there's probably wild orgies and free flowing drugs."

"Which I don't do," Roger snapped. "I've *never* done drugs, *never* had sex with Brock Hardwood in *or out* of the movies. And I've exclusively been with Tomas for the past month. So what *are you* implying?" He crossed his arms and stared defiantly at Barden.

Barden flipped his notebook closed and eagle-eyed the two boys in front of him. Young tanned, athletic. Everything he wasn't. "Then tell me this, if you weren't involved with Brock Hardwood, why would he have a photo of pretty boy here in his pocket?" He held the picture of Tomas face down on a fur rug with a man coming in from behind. The look on Tomas's face in the photo was of pure pleasure. In real life, standing before the Detective, it was pure astonishment. "Mr Stephanpopolopolous, why would Hardwood have a picture of the two of you doing that?"

"That's not Hardwood behind him, it's me." Roger was angered. "That's a scene from our second movie together, *Mount Cockmore.* As I *said,* Detective, we've been together exclusively for a month. I don't do movies with anyone but Tomas, and he doesn't do them with anyone but me. Is that clear?"

"And again." Barden waved the photo. "Why would he have a photo of Tomas being mounted on him? Did he have a crush? Was he in love with him? Had the two of them been in a movie together? Was Hardwood in this movie with the two of you?"

Silence.

"And there you have it." Barden leant back on his heels.

"He was an extra," Tomas said quietly, clinging to Roger's arm. "But we had no intimate scenes together. Just a party scene."

"Just a party scene. Was this the party?" He waved the photo again.

"No," Roger snapped. "Now we've answered your questions. I need to get back to work." He walked away and pulled Tomas with him, only stopping when the coroner carried Brock's body away.

"What was it like?" Tomas asked, his head following the stretcher being carried out.

"What?"

"Finding the body. What was it like?"

Roger sighed and pulled up his jeans. "Not fun."

"Everyone, may I have your attention," Violet called out. "Please gather round." She waited for the cast and crew to quieten down. "Go home. None of us will be in the right frame of mind for working tonight, and we're probably still in shock, so please, head home, and come back tomorrow." She moved to Marcus's side. He was dazed, moving his head from side to side, and she led him away to their office.

"Not much to do here then," Roger said, eyeing the set where he'd found Brock's body.

"I don't know what I'd do if I found a dead body," Tomas said. "Did anyone say how he died?"

Roger shook his head. "There was no blood, just a bit of powder on his nose."

"Another overdose?"

"Possibly."

"So, what do we do? Go home? Go out to dinner?"

"I couldn't eat."

"You okay?"

"Not really."

"We could just go home."

"No, I…" Roger's gaze wandered. "I need to…I need to get out of here. I'll see you at home." He took off for the car park.

"Roger," Tomas yelled and ran after him, but he was already jumping into his car. "Roger." He slapped the trunk as he took off. "Jesus!" He stood with his hands on his hips. "What the hell?"

"What the hell indeed, Mr Stephanpopodopolous."

"It's Steph-an-op-oul-os. *Nothing else.* It's not that hard to get right, Detective." He suspiciously eyed Barden. "I thought you were all gone."

"Not yet," Barden said. This wasn't his first foray into porn movies, or dealing with fags strung out on coke. He'd been around a while, working hardcore cases involving death, murder, suicide, and now dealing with the same movie production company. Coincidence? He wasn't sure.

"What are you still doing here?"

"Just wrapping things up." He flicked his pen against his notebook. "I see lover boy has left without you."

"He's upset. What do you expect? He found a dead body and needs to deal with that."

"Well, then maybe *you* can help me."

"With what, Detective? What could *I* possibly help *you* with when I turned up just a short time ago? When *you* were already here."

"How well did you know Hardwood?"

"What?" Tomas sighed, wanting to rush after Roger instead of being here with some dumb detective.

"How well did you know Hardwood? Have you talked a lot, about what, did you know he did drugs? Did he know Jeff Fastwater? Have you all worked together? I'm trying to find out why your co-workers are overdosing, Mr Steph-an-op-oul-os," he spelt it out.

"Maybe it's a bad batch of drugs," Tomas replied. "I

need to go." He headed for his car, but Barden followed.

He wasn't about to give up. "Have you ever done drugs, Mr Steph-an-op-oul-os?"

Tomas reached his car and turned. "No, Detective Barden, I haven't, and no, I didn't know Brock and Jeff did. And no, I don't know why they had photos of us on them. I have no idea what's going on. Now if that's all?" He waited with his hand on the car door handle.

"I'll definitely be in touch, Mr Steph-an-op-oul-os."

Tomas drove home, keeping an eye out for Roger, but he didn't find him. And he wasn't at home when he got there. Keeping an eye out for anyone suspicious, he went up to their apartment and locked the door behind him. Checking the place, he found no Roger and no intruder. "Jesus, where are you?"

He sat on the couch to watch TV, and come morning, when he woke, Roger still wasn't home. Making breakfast, he called Bette to let her know he wouldn't be doing the morning sessions and waited. Hearing the clunk of keys in the lock at eleven, he unchained the door just as Roger shoved it open. "Hey." He held the door. "God, you look awful."

Roger breathed in deeply. "Yeah well, I *feel* awful." He dumped his keys on the side table and slumped on the couch.

"Do you want some coffee?" Tomas wandered into the kitchen, watching Roger from the other side of the island bench.

"No, thanks. I've had way too much already this morning."

"Where were you?" Tomas asked tentatively. "I waited up for you. You didn't come home." He curled up beside Roger.

"I stayed with a friend." Roger rubbed his eyes. "Ugh, too bright."

"Which friend?"

"What does it matter?"

"It matters in case I need to get in contact with you, or something happens to you and I know where to find you."

"Like I said, with a friend."

Silence.

"A gay friend?" Tears sprang to Tomas's eyes as he feared the worst. "Were you drinking? Did you stay with a man?"

"Are you kidding me?" Roger asked, peering out from under his hand that shielded his eyes from the light. "Are you accusing me of sleeping with someone else?"

"No, I-"

"You what? Want to get all possessive like a woman and demand to know where I am at all hours? *And so what if I did get drunk?* Big fucking deal. Considering I found a dead body is it any wonder I needed a drink? Jesus." He lay down. "I didn't come home for this shit."

Tomas choked back a sob. "Then why did you bother coming home at all?" He stormed into the bedroom and grabbed his gym bag. "I'm going to work. You can sort your own shit out."

Roger finally realised what he had done. "Tomas," he called as he headed for the door. "Tomas." The door slammed. "Fuck!"

Tomas didn't go to work. He couldn't, not in the state he was in, so he went to the beach and sat crying in his car. After a while, there was a knock on the window. He looked up into the aqua eyes of his first lover. "Luiz?" He wound down the window.

"Tomas, my love. How are you? Long time no see." Luiz knew he had to keep it casual otherwise it would all be for nothing.

"Ah, yeah." Tomas wiped his face. "I didn't know you were still here in Miami."

"Yeah, well, I had been with Bertha here remember, so it is my home. What about you?"

"Yeah, yeah, doing okay, having a great time. At least I was until today."

Luiz leant against the car. "It looks like it." He motioned to Tomas's face. "Except for all the tears."

Tomas sighed and turned away.

"Lovers' quarrel?"

He looked back. "How do you know?"

"A guess. You said everything was okay until today, so it must be personal. You *have* been seeing someone…haven't you?"

Tomas blinked and shifted uncomfortably. "Yeah, yeah I have."

"And he's not treating you well?" Oh, how he wanted to take Tomas into his arms and hold him and love him and fuck him inside and out. His cock ached for him and strained inside of his shorts.

"He's…treated me fine. It's just…" He wasn't sure how much he should mention to Luiz since he'd left him back in Mykonos.

"Just what?"

"Just that he found a co-worker dead on the floor at work yesterday and it's really freaked him out. We were both short with each other this morning."

"Jesus, Tomas. Are you all right? You weren't hurt or anything were you?" He lightly touched his fingers to Tomas's shoulder. The sizzle was still there.

Tomas moved his shoulder to dislodge the fingers. "No. I wasn't hurt. I wasn't around when he died, or when Roger found him. But it was horrible, and must have been even worse finding the body."

"Wow, what happened?"

Tomas launched into the whole story, and Luiz listened intently. "It must have been rough on him, but he had no right to freak you out by staying out all night and not telling you. Talk about selfish."

"No. I get it," Tomas said. "I saw the body being carried away, and I saw another co-worker overdose at a party a few days ago, and that was upsetting, so I get it. He needed time to decompress."

"And he did that with alcohol and sex? Not a very good boyfriend."

"He didn't," Tomas cut in. "He got drunk and stayed with his friend instead of driving home drunk."

"He could've called you to pick him up. But he didn't bother calling you at all?" Luiz asked him. "Some boyfriend you've got. Can't even tell you where he is. Couldn't care less if you were worried."

"That's not the way it was."

"Do *you* know the way it was?"

"Yes...I..." Tomas sighed. "That's all I got out of him before I left."

"You left your boyfriend? After he comes home from an all-night bender doing God knows what with God knows who. I would have stayed and had it out with him. No man does that to me. I would've made him tell me every little thing and then kicked his sorry ass to the kerb."

"Roger's not like that. He wouldn't cheat and neither would I. We'll sort it out."

"Meanwhile, you're sitting here at the beach crying your eyes out. Yeah, great relationship you two have." He heard Tomas's silence and saw the sad expression. "How about we go for coffee? There's a little café across the street. If you want to talk about it..." He shrugged.

"No, no, but...I could do with a coffee."

They sat for two hours talking about Miami and Tomas's life in it. What Luiz had been doing, back working in the same gym as before, and talking about the spate of deaths, thefts, and their break-in.

"Someone broke into your home?" Luiz asked, shock sliding over his face. He had to keep it real after all.

"Yeah. Roger forgot to chain it, and the person got in."

"Did he steal anything?"

"No, just took pictures." Tomas sipped his coffee.

"Pictures of what?"

"Us."

"Us? You and Roger?"

"Yep."

"Doing what?"

"Having sex in bed." Tomas quickly looked away and buried his head in his coffee.

"You what? He what?"

"He was taking pictures of us in bed."

"Jesus." Luiz pretended to be oh so shocked while seething inside. "The gall of the man."

"Yeah. What a perve. It was horrible. You're in the midst of having sex, and you hear a camera going off and see a man at the end of your bed."

"It must have been so scary. Did you feel violated?"

Tomas thought about it. "Yeah, kinda. And then to have another death on top of it." He sighed. "It hasn't been a good week."

"No, it hasn't," Luiz agreed.

Tomas checked his watch. "I'd better go. I've got afternoon classes. Thanks for the coffee." He got up. "It was…nice to see you again. Good luck with everything." He walked past Luiz and out the door.

Luiz threw money down on the table and followed, watching as Tomas got into his car and drove off. He put his hand up to wave goodbye, but Tomas didn't acknowledge it. He lowered his hand. *So, Roger boy left Tomas out in the cold last night, all on his little lonesome. If only poor little Tomas knew what his beloved Roger got up to. Naughty, naughty.*

*****

Tomas arrived at Bette's in time for lunch, and told her all about his fight with Roger and running into Luiz.

"I hope he doesn't suck you in like last time. Stay away from him," Bette said over lightly baked lemon salmon and delicately boiled potatoes and asparagus. "He's bad news for you, Tomas."

"I know." Tomas sipped crystal water from a crystal glass. "We just talked about what's happened since being here in Miami."

"Including his running into us at *Sexe et Faveurs*?"

"Oh." His face fell. "I'd forgotten about that. Because I haven't seen him since, and so much has happened, I'd forgotten."

"Well, I bet *he* hasn't." Bette sipped her champagne. It was champagne all the time, any time of the day, morning, noon and night for Bette. She lived on the stuff, and only the best would suffice. "I bet he remembered every little moment you were together and still wishes he had it again."

"That's not the feeling I got today. He's back at the gym he used to work at, and he seemed okay. He didn't try anything with me."

"Just as well. You don't want him to ruin your relationship with Roger, do you? That would be such a pity if you did all because of a scoundrel like Luiz Manning. You stay away from him, Tomas. I have a feeling in my waters that he's up to something bad."

Tomas laughed. "You and your waters. I'm going to get ready for our first session." He turned to Webster. "Delicious as always."

Webster nodded his appreciation.

The rest of the day sped by quickly. The women wanted to talk about Tomas and his movie career, the latest death, and how they were dealing with it. All gave him advice on how to talk to Roger, leaving him more confused than he was that morning. He rolled into the studio car park at seven and found Roger on set getting everything ready. Biting his lip as he nervously walked over to him, he watched for some form of emotion. "Hey."

Roger looked up. "Hey." His attention turned back to the table he was fixing.

"Are we going to talk about it?"

"Nope."

"At all?"

"Nope."

"You're kidding?"

"Do I look like I'm kidding?" Roger asked, placing a lamp on the table and moving a chair.

Tomas huffed. "No, but then I guess I was kidding myself thinking I was ready to move in with you and have a relationship." He stormed off.

"Tomas," Roger called. "Ah, Jesus."

Marcus had been eyeing the whole thing. "Problems?"

"No!" Roger spat. "Just leave it."

"Will it interfere with your work later?"

Roger sighed. "I dunno." He stormed off in the opposite direction to Tomas.

An hour later, they were both on set ready to perform. You could have cut the tension with a knife, and the awkwardness between them was palpable. They stood on opposite sides of the set not looking at each other and trying to ignore everyone else.

"Take your places," Marcus yelled, sitting in his chair. "I hope you two drop the crap when the cameras roll. In three, two, one, action."

Roger and Tomas worked their lines, did their actions, and came together as they were supposed to. Albeit awkwardly and childishly. There was no chemistry, no zing, no whiz-bang between them and finally, Marcus called cut.

"What the hell is wrong with you two? What's happened to fuck you up?"

"Ask Roger, coz I sure as hell don't know." Tomas grabbed the blanket from the bed and wrapped it around himself. "And he sure as hell isn't telling me." He sat down with a flounce.

"Dencott? What the fuck is going on? Time is money."

Roger stood to attention with his hand on his hips, naked in front of all. "Nothing."

"Bullshit."

"A guy died here. *A co-worker.* And we all just move on as though it didn't happen and it only just happened three days after Jeff. It's freaking the fuck out of me," Roger yelled.

"And now we're getting to the root of the problem," Marcus said. "We're *all* freaked out. I've got two dead actors to replace. How do you think *I* feel? It's *not just you*, it's *all of us.* We've lost two family members and now have to replace them. But I have no time to sob and whine, we have to get on with it, and that *includes you.*"

"But I'm the one who found the body."

"That includes you," Marcus repeated. "Now sort

your shit out so we can get on with it. Time is money. You've got five minutes; sort your shit out *now!*" The crew left the sound stage and they were alone.

"Tomas."

"Roger."

Roger sighed. "I'm sorry. This is all my fault." He sat next to Tomas on his side of the bed. "I'm sorry. I just…haven't been handling any of this well."

"It's understandable."

"Yeah?" Roger looked at his lover. "Then explain it to me coz I don't know where I went wrong."

Tomas covered Roger's hand with his. "You found a dead person. That would have freaked anybody out. And you clearly haven't been dealing with that well, which is *understandable.*"

Roger moved his head slowly. "I can't believe another one is dead. First Jeff, now Brock, ugh." He buried his head in his hands. "Ah, I haven't been dealing with this and getting drunk didn't help." He sat up and grabbed Tomas's hand. "I'm sorry. I'm sorry I took off. I'm sorry I didn't call. I'm sorry I snapped at you. I'm sorry I didn't tell you I was staying at Freddy's."

Relief washed over Tomas. "You were at Freddy's? Why didn't you tell me?"

Roger shrugged a shoulder. "It wasn't a big deal. I was drunk, and knew I wasn't going to be driving, so Freddy let me bunk in his spare room. I didn't think that was a big deal."

Tomas rolled his eyes. "It isn't. *You not calling* to tell me all of this *is.* I was worried. If I'd known you were sleeping it off, I wouldn't have been."

Roger had the decency to look ashamed. "Yeah, fair enough. I'm sorry. I really haven't dealt with this well, have I?"

"Nope." Tomas smiled. "So, while we're sharing, I went to the beach this morning after our fight for some air, and Luiz popped up."

Roger stared incredulously. "You're kidding? *He's still here? In Miami?* I thought he'd buggered off after that club incident."

"So did I, but no. He's still here. We went across the road to a café and had a coffee. I left a couple of hours later."

"How was he?"

Tomas exhaled. "He *seemed* okay. Didn't go on about what had happened. We talked about our jobs, being here in Miami. He *really* seemed okay."

"That's a strange one then. Should make sure it's the only time you see him if he's that much of a weirdo. Are we okay, though?" He kissed Tomas's hand.

Tomas smiled at the gesture. "Of course we are. Just please tell me in the future so I know you're safe and I don't have to worry, *especially* since some weirdo broke into our apartment."

Roger nodded. "Fair enough." He gazed into his lover's eyes. "I love you. And I was such a dickhead. I'm sorry."

"I love you, too. And yes, you *were* a dickhead. Apology accepted."

"Good to see you two worked out your lovers' tiff. Now, let's get back to work," Marcus bellowed from his director's chair.

They turned to see everyone back at their stations.

"Better get back to work," Roger said, and they got into position.

"Okay boys, take it from the top. Three, two, one, action."

Roger cornered Tomas in the fake bedroom set. His fingers trailed up Tomas's arm to his shoulder and down his lean torso to his cock. They stroked, massaged, held, while lips and tongues continued in slow motions. Roger led him to the bed and laid him down across the fur cover. He lay on top, kissing his way up Tomas's body to his mouth, delighting in touching and tasting.

Tomas closed his eyes and arched upward as Roger invaded his neck, sucking him like a vampire, thirsty after a thousand years of drought. "Ah," he breathed, sliding his hand up Roger's side. "Ah…"

Roger made his way down and enveloped him, getting a hard sucking in of breath in return. The fake fireplace and overhead heaters made the room hot and steamy as Roger lay between Tomas's legs, leaning up on one arm while his hand joined the two of them together.

Tomas's left hand joined in while his right held onto Roger's arm. Their hands wrapped around their muscles, slowly rubbing them together, bringing their balls into the fray with back and forth motions.

Roger moved in slow fluid rocks so his package pushed against that of the man beneath him. He breathed. It always exhilarated him to touch his lover in this way, on screen and off. To see Tomas beneath him, lithe, lean, and in such perfect paradise made his heart pound and his cock hard. He kept control of himself. Small thrusts against his lover's testicles, his hand rubbing one cock against the other, fingers slid around the other's.

He watched Tomas close his eyes and arch, his breath coming in small gasps as they both approached climax. Roger moved a little faster, with longer, harder thrusts and Tomas lifted his legs to wrap around his lover's waist.

Roger slid over him and thrust until the end. Staring down, he watched Tomas's face. With the few lovers he'd had, none were like Tomas. Exotic, beautiful, perfect. The most amazing, giving, taking lover he'd ever had. His fingers slid up his body, up his neck and to his cheek, and Tomas opened his eyes as Roger extended fully onto him, his face above his lover's. *I love you,* he mouthed.

I love you, too, Tomas mouthed back, and Roger took him in a kiss.

Marcus knew better than to yell cut at a moment like this, so he silently got out of his chair and waved the crew away. They often let them go, the end result was always hotter than when they'd done the deed as they always did it again or more. They made for great extras on the video. He glanced back and saw them still joined in the throes of passion and wrapped around each other as they went full on into it. He left them to it, knowing Roger would deal with the cameras when they were done.

"Ah," Tomas gasped against his lover's mouth. "Oh, God, come, come inside me."

Roger moved in perfect rhythm until he gave Tomas what he asked for, and he covered his mouth with his own. They kissed, not letting go, not parting until they were done when they lay still in the quiet.

"I see Marcus and the crew have left." Roger gazed out over the sound stage as his fingers lazily made their way up and down Tomas's side.

A huge sigh of contentment left Tomas. "They always do. They know it's better to just leave us alone as they get better footage."

"Mmm," Roger murmured against Tomas's cheek as he nuzzled his way down to his collar bone and onto his nipple. "Mmm." He buried his face on Tomas's chest. "Mmm."

Tomas slid his hand over Roger's back while the other held his head there. "How long do you want to stay?"

Roger kissed his way across the splendid layer of dark hair to his other nipple. "Forever."

Tomas smiled. "We can't stay here forever. Although, all night could work." His hand slid down between them and squeezed. "How about now?"

Roger's head shot up. "What about forever?" He devoured Tomas for the rest of the night.

*****

Tomas made it to Bette's the next day where all of the ladies were pleased to know he'd sorted things out with Roger. "You'll soon know how well we got back together when *Big Cock Avalanche* comes out. That's the movie we made last night."

"Hot is it?" Marie asked. "How do you feel about doing the same with women?" She stretched her legs by spreading them apart as she sat on the ground. "I'm very flexible and *love* cocks."

Tomas blushed, swallowed and looked away. "I'm sure you do, Marie. But we're not interested."

"Shame." She moved into the splits. "Very flexible," she added.

"Don't worry about Marie," Bette said. "She's a whore from way back."

"Aren't we all, darling?" Marie rolled onto her back with her legs still splayed. "I'm flexible because of *you,* Tomas."

"Oh, for Christ's sake!" Bette exclaimed. "Shut your damn legs *and* your mouth." She turned from Marie's shocked expression to Tomas. "I'm so glad the two of you worked it out."

Tomas smiled. "So are we, Bette. So are we."

*****

That night, Luiz walked into *Wood,* a local gay hangout. He knew Tomas and Roger wouldn't be there, as they were working, but a few of their co-workers were, and he spied Brent Woodcock on the floor dancing up a storm. Making his way around the room he kept an eye on Brent, who was dancing with another man, one Luiz didn't recognise. He also didn't see crew or staff that he knew personally so believed he was safe with what he was about to do.

Dancing his way through the crowd, he came up behind Brent. Moving with the crowd, he danced around the couple until he was behind the dancing partner and then eyed Brent off over the man's shoulder, making sure to keep contact at all times. He did this for half an hour, throwing little waves and smiles in Brent's direction. When Brent took a break, Luiz followed him into the bathroom, greedily eyeing off his cock while he took a leak.

Nine inches of glorious hard cock.

Nowhere near as big as Tomas, but it would have to do.

"My, Grandma, what a big cock you have," Luiz said playfully from beside him at the urinals.

Brent caught on to the meaning. "All the better to fuck you with, little red."

"Would you?" Luiz said breathlessly, forgetting about peeing and letting his hard-on free. "You're so hot and fuckable. I've seen your movies but never imagined I'd ever meet you in…the flesh…" He glanced down at the muscle still in Brent's hand. "It's magnificent."

It stiffened.

"It clearly likes compliments." Luiz reached out and gently touched it.

It hardened even more.

"And it clearly likes a man's hand around it." Luiz looked into Brent's green eyes. "What about its owner? Does he like having a man around it?" he breathlessly quivered. "Can *I* be around it?"

The next thing Luiz knew, Brent was hauling him out of the toilets, out the back door, into the alley and behind a dumpster. "Drop your pants," he demanded, and Luiz obediently obliged. He took it hard and fast as Brent entered, thrust a few times, and withdrew.

"Oh, God," Brent gasped. "That was good. Oh, God, that was good." He zipped up his pants, leant against the wall, and lit a cigarette. "Oh, I love quick fucks."

Luiz pulled his pants up. "What about long fucks? Mouth fucks? Blow job out of the question?" His fingers slid to Brent's crotch.

"Have at it," Brent said, and Luiz got to work.

No man could resist a blowjob. Getting your cock sucked was the best thing next to sliced bread. And if the person doing the job got it right, the man at the other end got everything he wanted and then some. But this time it was Luiz that wanted something. He withdrew his mouth.

"Mind if I have a drag?" He nodded at the cigarette in Brent's mouth.

He held it out for Luiz to inhale and then stuck it back in his mouth, watching while Luiz performed the trick of blowing smoke rings onto his penis. "Awesome," Brent crowed. "Do it again."

Luiz obliged and took another drag. Once the smoke was gone, he sucked Brent until they were both done. He wiped his mouth and got to his feet. "You into more than cigarettes?" He leant against Brent's six foot muscular frame. "I've got a stash of stuff in my car. Maybe we could go somewhere…private." Luiz's hand took hold of Brent and cajoled until he heard yes. "Good, let's go to your place."

Half an hour later, they were spread out on Brent's king-size fur-covered bed, in his well-furnished apartment. Luiz had just given Brent what he'd given him and was flat on his back next to the porn star.

Brent snorted more of the coke Luiz had brought. "This is good shit, man." He flung his head back. "Oh, God, this is good shit. Fuck me again. Give it to me up the ass again. Fuck me with that your sword of yours and give it to me *hard.*" He snorted another line, and Luiz obliged, reminding him to keep snorting throughout. He went slowly, allowing line after line to go down, and when Brent's body started jerking he finished off, and Brent lay dead.

Three down, more to go.

He withdrew, rolled Brent over, jerked him off until he came over the pictures Luiz held. Oh, yes, to a normal person it would look as if Brent had downed drugs and got it off over pictures of Tomas Stephanopoulos. A jilted lover? A spurned nobody? Who knew, but that's how the cops needed to see it.

Brent's dead eyes stared at the ceiling, his long golden-brown locks spread out around him, his right hand holding his penis, his left the photos. The drugs spread out beside him with vials, a mirror, razor, and sprinkling of coke all sat there waiting for the cops to find.

Luiz stared down at the scene and took photos. He walked around to make sure everything else was intact before dressing, singing a little ditty in his head as he went. *'How much wood could a Woodcock cock if a*

Woodcock could cock wood.'

With one final check and a wave goodbye, Luiz turned off the lights and left.

*****

Brent Woodcock was found three days later, after police had the real estate agent let them in. The smell hit them like a ten tonne brick in the face, and they found the body covered in flies, and God knows what else.

When Brent hadn't shown up to work for two days or returned calls, Marcus had called to report him missing. And now, this is what the cops found.

Detective Barden slowly walked into the bedroom, a handkerchief over his mouth, and stood at the foot of the bed. He looked down at the body of Brent Woodcock, porn star, and realised why boys like him got into movies like that.

Big dicks.

He felt his shrivel at the mere sight of it, and speaking of it, he noticed photos in the left hand. Sidestepping his fellow officers who all stood around checking out the view, Barden made his way to the side of the bed for a closer look at the photos. "Interesting."

"Sir?" one of the officers asked through his own handkerchief.

"Hurry up and get the coroner here. I want these photos cleaned and packed up." He quickly covered his mouth again.

"Sir." The officer couldn't wait to get out into the fresh air and neither could Barden.

"Everyone out until the coroner's done," he yelled. "Tape the door shut and put two guards on it. No one enters until the coroner does."

An hour later, the coroner was done.

"Same as the last two," he said, putting his instruments in his bag. "Drug overdose."

"Which is obvious," Barden said.

"It looks that way, but won't be confirmed until autopsy. I'll give you the details in a couple of days, Jeremiah." He slapped him on the shoulder in passing.

"Thanks, Doc." Jeremiah Barden thought he'd seen it all, yet now he had a spate of porn star deaths on his hands. Ah, if only the good old days still existed. He picked up the Ziploc bags and put each photo separately into them. "Don't want to get them all covered in juice." He took one last look and let the coroner's people do their jobs.

*****

Two days later, Barden had three files on his desk. Three files containing cases of three porn stars all dead of apparent overdoses. All had sex beforehand. But then what did one expect from men who fuck for a living. And all three had copious amounts of cocaine in their systems. The reports on the cocaine had it at D-grade level. Not so much coke, but a whole bunch of other stuff mixed in with it. Ecstasy, laundry powder…some had bleach and a bunch of other stuff Barden couldn't even pronounce. He hadn't come across this kind of coke before, although, it wasn't the first time he'd seen impure cocaine.

It was time to talk, and he knew who to.

Twenty minutes later, he stood in the studios of *Seralift Productions*. "Mr Seralift, three of your stars are dead. All of them from drug overdoses. All had sex before or during, so someone else is involved and that's why I need to question you all."

"About what?" Marcus bellowed. "Whether they get drugs from me? Was I the one to give it to them? I don't run my place that way; we are clean cut, and everyone found doing drugs is automatically fired." He paced up and down in front of Barden. "You can get your attack dogs in here; you will *not* find coke or any other drug in my studios, including in lockers and change rooms."

"How well did you know Mr Woodcock?" Barden asked, closely watching Seralift's expression.

"As well as can be expected," Marcus huffed. "I check their credentials, hire them, and make movies. That's all I have to do with it."

"Do you sample them, Mr Seralift?"

"Sample what?" Marcus stopped and stared the man down. "Sample what, Detective?"

"Your workers'…*credentials*." Barden remained unblinking. Marcus Seralift was not about to get the better of him. He'd dealt with far worse.

"I do not fuck my stars," Marcus bellowed, realising everyone in the studio had turned to watch. He lowered his voice. "I don't fuck them. I don't supply them, and I certainly don't allow them to do drugs. *You got that!"*

Barden backed off. "Fine. I want to talk to Dencott, he here?"

Marcus turned. "Over there. Dencott, get over here."

Roger warily wandered over. "What now?"

"Brent Woodcock died in his apartment a few days ago. He was found holding photos." He held up a bag with the photo in it. "It seems he had ah…" He cleared his throat. "Masturbated over them."

Roger screwed up his face. "Ew, God." He looked at the photo and saw Tomas with a cock in his mouth.

"Any ideas, Mr Dencott?"

Roger sighed and took a closer look, finally giving a shrug. "It could be from one of our movies."

Barden cocked a brow. "You don't know?"

"As I told you last time, Detective, Tomas and I are exclusive. We only star with each other in movies, no one else. So it has to be me he's deep-throating."

"Mmm," Barden mumbled. "Why would Woodcock be getting off over pictures of Stephanopoulos? He's *your* boy isn't he?"

Roger crossed his arms. "He's my *partner* if that's what you meant."

"Yeah…that's what I meant. So why would Woodcock have photos of lover boy and why did he masturbate over them?"

"Look, I don't know. We only knew each other through work and haven't worked together for months now," Roger growled.

"You worked together?" Barden eyed him suspiciously. "In what capacity?"

Roger rolled his eyes to the ceiling and threw his

arms down beside him in frustration. "We made a couple of movies together. Fucked in them. Happy now?"

"So, Woodcock could be jealous that you have a new toy boy?"

"I highly doubt it," Roger said. "We worked in the movies, nothing happened in real life."

"Didn't date, or fuck for fun after the cameras stopped rolling?"

"No," Roger snapped. "I'm done talking, Detective." He stormed off backstage leaving Barden alone.

*****

Luiz watched the scene unfold from the shadows. *Poor Roger, feeling the heat from the detective. Well, three deaths are on your shoulders and there's more to come. So get ready, Roger, the fun is about to blow you away.*

He watched Barden leave and followed in the shadows, spying Roger sneaking out to his car and taking off in the opposite direction.

Luiz hurried to his own car out on the street and took off after Roger. "Now where's he going?" he muttered, following Roger all the way to Brent Woodcock's apartment building and watched him park in an alley and make his way inside. Fifteen minutes later, Roger came out and left, driving off to Brock Hardwood's place.

Luiz parked down the street. *Now, this is getting interesting.*

He watched Roger run in the back way and emerge fifteen minutes later. And off he went to Jeff Fastwater's house, and once again, fifteen minutes later, he was in and out.

All three places. I wonder what he's up to. He followed Roger out to the Glades where he watched him stop by a waterway, get out, look around, and rip something up into a million pieces and throw it into the water. Luiz waited until Roger had left, then went in search of those million pieces. Once he'd collected all he could, he went back to his motel room and spread the pieces out on the table. It took him the rest of the afternoon to put the photos back together. There were twelve altogether, and in four were Roger and Brent.

"Ah, interesting," Luiz muttered. Roger in compromising positions with all three men. Pulling out a roll of tape, he stuck them together and examined them closer. *Very* compromising positions. *Now, was that in their movie or after hours?* He studied them, trying to remember if the sets were stages at the studio. *Not that I remember.* He glanced over his own photos, but none of the sets looked the same.

"Ah, after hours. Well, well, well. I bet he doesn't want lover boy or Detective Barden seeing these." No, no, no. If anyone saw these photos, Roger's life would be over. Suspicion would fall squarely on his shoulders, and he'd be put in the spotlight for the three deaths. Oh, yes, it would all fall squarely on Roger's shoulders, and Tomas would have no choice but to leave him and come back to me. Oh, yes, he will come back to me.

*****

Barden sat behind his desk staring at the files. They were spread out, along with photos, reports, and a whole pile of witness statements. And what did he have to go with them?

Zip. Zilch. Nada.

His cop instincts told him there was more to this than overdoses. There was sex, there was porn; they were all from the same production house. Something extremely fishy was going on here, and he couldn't put his finger on it. He checked the list of people involved and decided to do some digging.

Two hours later, he had a list of felonies and reports involving most members of *Seralift Productions*, from misdemeanours to jail time. The studs of the *Seralift* stable had pasts as bad boys. And one report, in particular, intrigued him.

It was the report of a Mustang convertible being trashed back in August. It seemed Mr Dencott had some bad luck, then there was the spate of thefts he'd heard about when eavesdropping…not that they were newsworthy. Little things, personal items, photos, jewellery had gone missing at the studios, and now there were three deaths.

An idea started forming in his mind. Either someone was out to destroy *Seralift*, or someone was out to deal with the stars of the productions.

Why would you want to kill porn stars unless you were some kind of religious zealot who hated fags? If straightening them out didn't work, killing them did? That was some mentality. He wrote the theory in his notebook.

The next angle to investigate was why did all three have pictures of the new kid Stephanopoulos? He was a good looking rooster, new to the game, but had kept to himself. Yet here were all three dead studs with pictures of him. Did they take them or did someone else take them…oh…someone else took them. But who?

He went back over the list of employees past and present, all the way back to the very beginning of *Seralift* and their manly productions. "Anthony De Milo, Cade Caldwell, Evan Williams, Luiz Manning, Nick Michaels, Roger Dencott, Van Michaels," he muttered at random down the list. Plus new boy Tomas, the three dead, and a bunch more. Jesus, they went through them like he went through underwear. What was their secret?

He tried connecting names with Tomas, but except for Roger, he couldn't. Stephanopoulos was new in town, and Dencott had just passed his two year status. The rest had been around for years. Unfortunately, the dots just weren't connecting, and he needed fresh air.

*****

Tomas didn't eat much at Bette's the next day. The morning sessions were slow, and now he wasn't hungry. There was something going on in the pit of his stomach, and he didn't know what. His energy was down, and his taste buds were flat. He pushed his plate away.

"Not hungry?" Bette cut a piece of succulent chicken breast with lemon butter sauce and roasted cashews. Three small garlic butter potatoes were the side dish.

"No." He took a sip of juice and leant back in his seat. "I don't feel…like I normally do." Closing his eyes, he took a slow deep breath.

"Are you sick?" She gazed at his face. "Your colour isn't up to snuff."

A slow exhale. "I'm not sure. I don't feel like I normally do. A bit down." He shook his head. "Something… I don't know, I can't put my finger on it."

"Maybe you're coming down with something?"

"Maybe, although, I don't get sick."

"Ever?"

"Not since I was a kid."

"Maybe you ate something that didn't agree with you?"

"Yeah, maybe."

But that evening he stumbled into the studios.

"Whoa, take it easy tiger." Roger caught him. Noticing the pale colour and weakness, he helped him over to Marcus's chair "You okay? Have you eaten?"

"Not since breakfast." Tomas collapsed. "Ugh, I don't feel well."

"You don't look good either." Roger checked his eyes. "We need to get some food into you, and you need a good night's rest."

"What the hell!" Marcus bellowed. "Get that germy-looking kid out of my chair. Do I need to disinfect it now?" He stared at Tomas. "Ain't no way you're working tonight. Take the night off and if you're not better tomorrow take the rest of the week off. Roger, get him home."

"Come on, you." Roger hauled him to his feet. "I'll get you home." Leaving Tomas's car in the lot, Roger drove home and tucked him into bed. "I'll go and get you some hot soup from down the road." Fifteen minutes later he was back, and Tomas was downing chicken soup and dumplings.

"Feel better?" Roger sat beside him on the bed eating Moo Shu pork.

Tomas thought. "Yeah, I do. My stomach's got food in it. I'm getting some strength back. I feel okay."

"Well, try not to go without food again. Your blood sugar must have been low. You need to keep your strength up. Finished?" He collected the rubbish.

"Yeah. There's enough left for tomorrow, so don't throw it out." Tomas stuck the lid back on. "Put it in the fridge."

"Don't waste anything do you?" Roger said, heading into the kitchen. He chucked the rubbish and put the soup in the fridge. "Jesus, the milk's hit its use by date, better throw that out." He poured it down the drain and threw the carton into the bin. "Hey, you'll need a new milk tomorrow," he said, walking back into the bedroom where he saw Tomas fast asleep. Pulling the covers up around his shoulders, he kissed him on the cheek and whispered, "Sweet dreams, my sweet prince."

*****

The next morning, Tomas felt better, so they had breakfast at a local café. At work, everyone noticed how much better he looked.

"You've got your colour back *and* your appetite," Bette said over lunch.

Tomas nodded. "I do. I feel good again, so maybe it *was* a bad meal."

"It certainly wasn't from here." Bette laughed.

"Of course it wasn't," Tomas told her. "Geez Bette, I wouldn't know *what* to think if you were poisoning me," he joked.

"Oh, darling." She giggled delicately with a hand to her mouth. "Why would I kill you? You make me money."

*****

That night after work, Tomas and Roger grabbed some groceries from the local market before going home.

"I really don't know why you drink that stuff. It's unnatural," Roger commented on the homogenised, unflavoured, unsugared milk that Tomas was putting away.

"It's the healthiest milk there is," he replied. "How do you think I stay in such great shape? By having healthy milk in healthy cereal every morning!"

"God, I don't know how you do it," Roger complained as he sat on the stool under the island bench. "You eat so healthily it's sickening."

Tomas pulled a face. "But *you* certainly don't mind reaping the rewards."

Roger frowned. "What rewards?"

"The reward that is my long, lean cock that all of those healthy foods go towards making."

"Yes," Roger agreed. "That is true. And I'd like to go and play with that cock now."

From the shadows on the street, Luiz watched the living room light go out. He'd seen them buy their groceries and knew he had to go in again. Looking left and right, he slipped across the street and inside, up two flights of stairs and to their door. Sliding his key into the lock, he tried the door, glad that Roger had forgotten to chain it. Moving inside he went into the kitchen, removed the carton of milk, replaced it with one of his own, and quietly slipped back out with no one noticing he'd even been there.

He paused and breathed. He'd heard the sighs and giggles, the gasps and groans, and it absolutely killed him to hear it. He wanted Tomas all to himself and had to wait it out until he could make his move. But the time was coming and coming soon. So soon, in fact, it was just a day away.

*****

Tomas cracked open the milk the next morning and drank straight from it.

"We do have glasses, you know," Roger quipped. "They're those things there." He pointed to the ten clear glasses sitting on the kitchen shelf. "Or have you not seen one before? A glass I mean."

"Ha, ha." Tomas poured milk over his cereal. "I'm the only one who drinks it, so what does it matter?"

"True," Roger said, whipping up Eggs Benedict. "I'm not much of a milk lover anyway, so I'll leave that to you."

"You really should try it." Tomas offered the carton. "It's not that bad."

Pulling a face, Roger said, "No, thanks. I'll stick to my eggs and toast, and coffee straight and black."

"Clearly not how you prefer your men," Tomas teased.

Roger laughed. "Straight no, black, not so bad."

"You've had a black man?" Tomas's interest was piqued, having forgotten about seeing Roger working with a black co-star.

"Yes." Roger inhaled a whole forkful of eggs and wriggled his brows.

"So, it's clearly not true then."

Roger stopped eating long enough to ask, "What?"

"Once you've had black you never go back." Since Roger was Tomas's second, Luiz his first, he'd never been with a black man. Not even in a movie.

"I'm with you, so obviously not."

*****

Once the sun went down, Luiz put his plan into action. He was after another victim, and it had to be tonight. *Oh, yes,* he thought, *tonight it's all going down.* He made his way to *The Bat and Balls,* an

Aussie pub that catered to gay men. It was a few years old, had become a big hit with the locals, and was the place for gay Aussie men to hang out when they were in Miami.

Luiz walked through the door and looked around, spying the man he was after sitting with friends at a table. Pushing his red hair out of his face, he went up to the bar and ordered a beer. Keeping to himself as he casually looked around, he tried to remain inconspicuous.

"Anything else, mate?" the blond Aussie bartender asked.

Luiz looked him over. "How about you? You gay?"

The blond hunk laughed. "I am, but taken."

"Pity," Luiz commiserated. His gaze wandered around, noticed his target, and kept on wandering. *Have to play it cool and casual.* He checked out the décor, the brunet hunk at the end of the bar, and the black guys at the far table. *Mmm, black...* God, black men had great cocks, great big hulking pythons of love they were, but Tomas's was better.

The men saw him looking and gave him a nod. He gave a saucy cocked brow in return before turning his attention back to the man he was there for. The man looked in his direction and Luiz quickly looked away, blushing, before coyly looking back. The man was still staring; a smile on his face as he checked out what Luiz was packing in his tight jeans.

Luiz gave a coy shrug of the shoulder. The man kept staring. Luiz asked the bartender which way to the toilets, and with a glance over his shoulder, walked down the hall and into the small bathroom. He didn't have to wait long as the man soon followed.

Aiden Head had been with *Seralift* for two and a half years, not long before Roger started, and they had starred in a movie together. Now, Luiz wanted Aiden to star in *his* movie.

Aiden locked the door and leant against it. "I saw you checking me out."

"Was I?" Luiz murmured, slowly unzipping his pants.

Aiden eyed his crotch. "Yes. Yes, you were, and now I want to see what you've got." He moved over to Luiz, pushed him against the sink and finished unzipping his pants. Pulling it out, he moved it in his hands.

Luiz groaned, collapsing against the sink. "Oh, God, oh, God that's so good." He loved it when hands other than his own manipulated his cock. "Oh, God, fuck me."

"Not yet." Aiden unzipped and pulled his own out. "Let's get to know each other first." He pushed against Luiz and manhandled them both.

Luiz's hands joined in a mad frenzy of cockfighting. They thrust against each other in a mad dance of lust until each came.

"Ah," Aiden groaned, letting his head fall back. "Oh, God that was good."

"Is that all I get?" Luiz whispered, massaging Aiden's manhood until he hardened again. "Is that all I get? I want more. I want you. I want you to fuck me up the ass." He turned around and guided Aiden into him. "Now." Holding onto the sink with one hand he grabbed Aiden's right hand and brought it around to his package, rubbing it all over as Aiden thrust inside him. He was long, strong and powerful and hit all the right spots. They came in a frenzy at the bathroom sink.

Aiden finally stepped back, but Luiz grabbed his jacket. "I want more. I want more of you. I want you in my mouth, up my ass, inside of me. I want to be inside of you. Come with me, let's leave and go somewhere else." Luiz's hand slid down to Aiden's crotch. "Let's go somewhere where we can indulge all night."

Aiden stared glassily at the redhead in front of him. "I want you to fuck me too. Let's go." He zipped up, and they made their way out the back door. They barely made it to Aiden's car before they were fucking on the back seat like wild animals.

"Oh, God, oh, God." Luiz bounced up and down. He wrapped Aiden's hands around his cock, moving them up and down as Aiden thrust. "Oh, God, oh, God fuck me," he yelled. "Fuck me." They climaxed and relaxed. "Oh, God," Luiz panted. "You don't stop." He rolled onto his back, spread his legs and pulled Aiden down on him. "Can we make it to your place?" he whispered in his ear.

"We can try," Aiden whispered back and climbed over the seat to gun the engine. They made it to his place, up the stairs, and into the bedroom before ripping each other's clothes off and humping on the bed.

"Oh, God, oh, God," Luiz cried as he rammed it home. "Oh, God." He collapsed onto Aiden's back. "Oh, God, you're good. So, so, good. A big cock and a tight asshole just right for the taking."

"Take them all if you like. You're the best fuck I've

had in years." Aiden pushed up and moved so he was free of Luiz. Digging around in his bedside drawer he pulled out a small bong and lighter. "Want some?"

"No," Luiz said. "I've got my own shit if you want to give it a try?"

Aiden stopped puffing. "Like what?" He blew out smoke.

"Coke." Luiz fetched the small kit from his jacket pocket and brandished a vial. "Want some? It's good shit."

Aiden licked his lips. "I'll tell you what. You smoke this bong, lie back and enjoy, and I'll snort coke right off your cock."

Luiz sizzled inside. "Why fucking not?" He took the bong, lay back, and smoked while Aiden spread a line of coke along his dick. He snorted, he licked, he sucked.

Luiz groaned. "Oh, God, that's good." He was so relaxed he'd almost forgotten what he was there for. "Again."

Aiden spread, snorted, licked and sucked again, and Luiz held him there, enjoying the hot tongue around him. "Oh, God, you suck good. Oh, God." He felt himself coming. "Swallow, swallow, I'm coming. Oh, God, oh, God." He climaxed, and Aiden took it. "Oh, God, you're good. More coke?" He rolled Aiden onto his back and lay on top, sprinkling cocaine in Aiden's nose. Rocking back and forth, he felt the manly strength of the man under him. "You're so fucking hot," he murmured into his nipple. He bit and pulled. "So, fucking hot. More coke?"

He poured the rest of the vial into Aiden's nose and made his way down to his cock. He swallowed him whole. *So fucking good,* he thought, lost in dreamland, sucking on a cock as if he'd never had it before. When he was done, he moved back up and sat on it. "More coke? I have another vial." He moved up and down slowly. Oh, God, he was enjoying this. It was so, so good it seemed like such a pity to kill him. He looked at his watch. He had a few hours of play time left. And play he did, until Aiden was out of his mind on a drug overdose four hours later.

"Come on, baby, we're gonna take a trip." Luiz dressed and cleaned up, keeping all of the essentials within arm's reach. He wrapped Aiden in a robe and helped him down to his car, then quickly ran back up to grab his things. Glad that Aiden lived in a house and not an apartment.

He drove to Roger's building, quietly drove into the underground garage and left the car parked lengthways. Making sure no one was around; he slid over Aiden and opened the passenger door.

"Come on, baby. We're home now." He glanced around and checked his watch. He had a couple of hours until they started leaving for work and he had to be out of there now. He smacked Aiden's face to wake him up. "Come on, baby, time for another line of coke."

"Mmm," Aiden mumbled, struggling to wake.

"Come on, baby." Luiz unscrewed the three vials and tilted Aiden's head back, holding his mouth open while he tipped the powder in.

"Mmm." Aiden tried to struggle as Luiz held his

mouth shut, his eyes staring into his as the coke hit his adrenaline, dissolved, absorbed and sped to his heart. "Mmm." He grabbed Luiz's hand that was holding his mouth, but all he saw was black. His hands fell. He stopped struggling. All power left him.

Aiden Head was dead.

Four down, one to go.

Luiz quickly scratched, *Roger, I love you*, into Roger's car with Aiden's car key and then hauled his body out of the car and laid it between Roger's and Tomas's. He stuck a few photos of Tomas into Aiden's hand, opened his robe to display the whole package, and spread the coke vials around Aiden's body. He had to make it look like a suicide *or* murder. Either way, Roger was going to be hauled in for this one way or another.

He gathered his own things, wiped down the wheel and handles and anything else that might have his prints on it, and glanced at his watch. He saw it was five a.m. on the dot.

Because he'd cased the joint, he knew the first tenant left for work at six-thirty, so it would be just an hour and a half before Aiden was discovered. Tomas and Roger were up at seven, so only two and a half hours away. If only he could stick around and watch the festivities, but alas, he couldn't. Sneaking out of the car park, he silently ran a few streets then walked the rest of the way back to the pub where he'd left his car. It was five-thirty. Not long now.

*****

George Cauldwell was an average man.

Average in every sense of the word.

He was average height, average weight, average in looks, demeanour and stature. He had an average job in an average company, doing average things. But for the next two months, George Cauldwell would not be average at all.

George hit the alarm and threw back the covers. It was another average day in the Cauldwell home. Average décor, average life. He showered, put on his clothes for work, and had a breakfast of cereal, fruit and juice. All so average.

At six-twenty on the dot, George Cauldwell stepped outside his apartment, locked the door, and walked down four flights of stairs to get to his car in the underground park. He saw a black car parked in front of the two fags' cars and kept on walking. Unfortunately, it meant he was blocked in and wouldn't be able to back out of his parking space.

"Goddamn it," he swore and eyed the car. There was no one in it, and the passenger side was open.

Walking around the back of the car, he spied a slipper and then a foot. And coming to a stop between the two fags' cars, he saw the body that foot belonged to; a gorgeous above-average young man with a tight torso and a big dick.

George Cauldwell stared at the man's body. He'd dared not look at a naked one for the last two years, had been too afraid of the feelings it stirred up, but now, one was on full display, right there in front of him, in *his* parking garage.

"Sir, sir, are you all right?" he called while eyeing off the cock and balls and licking his lips. Oh, how he wanted to touch it, feel it, taste it. "Sir." He leant down to feel for a pulse at the neck; the beautiful long neck that belonged to the beautiful long body that provided him with the beautiful long cock that his eyes wandered over.

He hovered inches above it. The beautiful long cock that looked so delicious he could taste its sweetness. His tongue peeked out to wet his lips and kept on going until George Cauldwell had that juicy long cock in his mouth.

Oh, my God, it's so good, he thought, sucking and tasting and licking. His average mouth left it behind and licked its way up the long beautiful body until it came to its mouth, where it tasted and licked and sucked. *Oh, my God I'm in heaven*. He sighed and decided he couldn't keep it in any longer.

Taking off his clothes, he lay full out on the dead body of Aiden Head. George Cauldwell didn't care that he was dead, just that he wasn't resisting.

After devouring the front of Aiden where he backed onto his dick and rubbed a dead man's hands over his ball sack, he rolled the body over and entered him from behind. "Oh, God, oh, God, you're so good," the very average George Cauldwell told the very above-average Aiden Head. "Oh, you're such a good fucker, so good." His hands explored every inch of Aiden's body and made Aiden's hands explore every inch of him. "Oh, God, you're so good."

George rolled Aiden back and rubbed his balls up

and down the long, strong torso of the young man beneath him. He lengthened out and went back to kissing the mouth, the mouth that now lay perpetually open in a frozen state. When he was finished tonguing a dead man, he sat on his face and put his cock in Aiden's mouth. "Oh, yes, suck it, suck it, oh, God, yes, suck it," George cried out. He moved Aiden's head in opposite motions, hardening and coming. "Oh, God, oh, God," the very average George Cauldwell cried.

He waited until the tingling died down before sitting backwards and taking Aiden up the back passage again. He enclosed Aiden's hands around him and rubbed as he moved on a dead man's dick.

His hands slid up and over his own body, touching himself, masturbating, fucking a corpse. In fact, if anyone had been watching the scene, it would have been a very crazy and debauched scene indeed. A man, very much alive, fucking a man that was very much dead, in between two cars with a third one parked across. Some people would have merely thought two fags were getting it off in the underground parking. To those that knew, which only two did, the scene would be seen for what it was.

And now there was about to be a third person to see the scene that way from the start, especially when it took him only an instant to realise what was actually going on.

The very average George Cauldwell came and slid down onto Aiden's body.

"Ahem."

George's head flew up into the shiny gold light of a

detective's badge. "Oh, my God," he cried and tried to cover himself.

"Detective Barden, Miami PD. What do you think you're doing?" He slid his badge back into his pocket, staring down at the naked middle-aged man on top of a dead body.

Oh, yes. The very average George Cauldwell was about to be very average no more. In fact, he was about to become very *non*-average. For the world would soon find out what a raving necrophiliac George Cauldwell was.

"I, ah…" George covered himself with his shirt. "It's not what it looks like."

Detective Barden smirked. "I'm sure it's *very much* what it looks like. You're a guy who fucks dead bodies. And now it's *my* dead body. Get up and get dressed." He watched while Cauldwell quickly put his clothes on and stood in front of him.

George saw the police car in the driveway and the two officers leaning against it. "Am I…under arrest?"

"Of course you are." Barden led him away. "You've disturbed a crime scene and had sex with a corpse." He turned Cauldwell around while he was cuffed. "Did you kill the corpse?"

"What? What, no, no." The very average George Cauldwell's eyes widened. "I didn't kill anybody. I just found him there…"

"And took advantage of the situation," Barden interrupted.

"No, no." George vehemently shook his head.

"Yes, yes," Barden replied. "And now I have a crime

scene. Take him away. I'll charge him later." He watched the very average George Cauldwell be placed into the back seat of the car, head shaking left and right, eyes wide as if he was on coke. He noted the pale complexion and short brown hair. Yep, it's always the average ones. He saw George stare out the back window as they drove away, then called for reinforcements. He walked back to the scene and crouched, spying vials under the cars. Turning his head to the right, he spied something on Roger's car. *Roger, I love you.*

"Well, well, well, and now we have a connection. How nice of him to spell it out for me." He checked his watch. Six-fifty. *Nah, we'll let the kids sleep some more.*

The ground crew and coroner rolled in ten minutes later. "Doc." He nodded. "Got another one."

The doctor looked down at the body. "The scene has been disturbed."

"Oh, it certainly has." Barden rocked on his heels, his hands in his pockets. "Found some perve having sex with the body."

Doc looked up in surprise. "You're kidding?"

"Nope."

"Jesus bloody hell, a necrophiliac!"

"Yep."

"I hope he didn't do too much damage." He set down his bag and opened it.

"Don't know. Hopefully, you can tell me if he did." Barden watched Doc pull out several instruments and kneel over the body.

Doc shook his head. "It's compromised." His eyes

found the vials under the car. "And full of drugs I take it." He used tweezers to pick them up and put them into an envelope. "I'll get them analysed." He noticed the scratching on the car. "Ah, got a suspect have we?"

"Dunno yet, Doc. I'll get 'em on the way out I suppose." He watched him finish up and cart the body away before examining the third car. "No wallet, no ID, nothing." He dug around in the glove compartment and found several business cards. *Aiden Head, Seralift Productions.* "Ah, Mr Head was a fag fucker. That tells me everything." He checked his watch. Seven-fifteen. Time for business. "Come with me." He motioned to two officers and made his way up to the second floor.

*****

Tomas and Roger were finishing up with breakfast. Roger with his eggs and toast, and Tomas with his cereal.

"What did you want to do this weekend?" Roger asked. "I thought we'd get away for a couple of days. We could head north or go out to one of the islands."

"Sounds good," Tomas said. "Do we get a holiday from the studio? It's nearly two months now, and we make movies most nights except for the weekends."

"And you work all day. You can give that up now you know. You're making good money. Do you really need to keep working out old ladies?"

"If it weren't for those old ladies I wouldn't be here," Tomas admonished him. "And *we* would not have met."

Roger pouted. "True, but you spend all day, every day with them. It's not for the money."

"I like training." Tomas dumped his bowl in the sink and turned around. Pain seared through his gut. "Ah." He grasped the kitchen counter. "Oh, God."

"Tomas." Roger ran around the island and held his lover. "What is it? What's wrong?"

"My stomach. Oh, God," Tomas gasped. "The pain."

Roger helped him to the sofa and sat beside him. "Is it left or right?"

"What?" Tomas gasped through the hazy fog.

"If it's your right side, it's your appendix."

Tomas screwed up his face in thought. "No, oh, uh, it's all over." He wrapped his arms tighter around himself and felt the pain subsided. "Oh, God, I think it's passing." He breathed in and out slowly as Roger rubbed his lower back.

Three knocks sounded on the door.

Roger's head flew to face the door and back, while his hand kept rubbing. "Are you okay yet?"

Tomas breathed and slowly unfurled. "Yeah. The pain's going. I'm okay."

"What the hell *was* that?" Roger asked, staring into the face of the man he loved.

Tomas didn't look good. His pallor was a little grey; eyes a little dull.

Three more knocks sounded on the door.

"Just a minute," Roger yelled, before turning back Tomas. "Someone's impatient."

"Go answer it, I'm okay." Tomas sat up and gently

stretched. "I'm okay."

Roger ran to open the door. "What," he barked before running back to the couch.

"Am I interrupting?" Barden asked, seeing a sick-looking Stephanopoulos and a doting Dencott on the couch.

"Yes, you are." Roger looked up. "Detective. What do we owe the pleasure to?" He kept rubbing Tomas's back. "Now's really not the time."

"So I see." He stood in front of them while the two officers waited at the door. "Not feeling well, Mr Stephanopoulos?"

"Not really," Tomas replied, warily eyeing the man off. "I've been off-colour for a while."

"Coming down with something?" Barden studied the two.

"Probably. Is there something you wanted?"

"Yes. Do either of you know Aiden Head?"

Roger's eyes narrowed. "Why?"

Barden noticed the change in Roger's expression. "Because he's dead."

"What!" Roger and Tomas said at the same time.

"Another one?" Tomas went on while Roger stayed quiet and looked away. "What happened?"

"Oh, the usual…drug overdose." Barden kept his eye on Roger until he looked up.

His eyes widened. "You don't suspect *me* do you?"

"Just asking if you knew him, Mr Dencott. He *does work* for *Seralift Productions*. Have the two of you made a movie together?" He watched closely.

Roger looked down. "Two years back after I first

started. It was only the one. That's all we ever did. We'd do a movie with one actor and move on to the next, so it wouldn't get stale."

"But that's not how you do things now. You've told me several times the two of you are *exclusive*." He glanced at Tomas who was looking strangely at Roger. "Are you telling me that's a recent development since Mr Stephanopoulos has joined the stable?"

Roger heaved a sigh. "That's what I'm saying. Marcus saw the chemistry between us and knew I never wanted to work with anyone else, so I suggested it to him that we make movies exclusively. After seeing the footage he got, he agreed wholeheartedly."

"I'm sure he did." Barden saw Tomas's eyes never leave Roger's. "That must make you feel...*special*, Mr Stephanopoulos. That you're...*exclusive*." He made the quote marks with his fingers.

Tomas finally looked up. "Ah, yeah, yeah it does. I don't think I'd be doing this if I wasn't working with just Roger. I wouldn't feel comfortable otherwise."

"Fucking other men?" Barden asked.

Tomas's eyes narrowed. "That's right."

"Had *you* met Aiden Head?" He kept his eyes trained on Tomas. "What was he like?" He rocked slightly on the balls of his feet.

Tomas shrugged. "Met him once in passing. He seemed okay."

Roger got to his feet. "What's the point in all of this, Detective? Every time one of our own has died you've come bearing photos. *So where are they now? Am I a suspect, or did Aiden just take too much blow?*

Why are you here?"

Barden produced the photos and held them up for the both of them to see.

Roger stared. "That one looks like the movie we did two years ago." He pointed to the one on the right of him deep-throating Aiden on the back seat of a car. He looked at the one on the left, of Tomas being taken in a classroom. "That could be our movie from last month."

"Yet, your face is not in the photo," Barden replied. "In fact, anytime there's a photo of Mr Stephanopoulos in the throes of passion with someone you claim is you, your head is cut out of it. Why would that be, Mr Dencott?"

Roger shrugged. "How the fuck would I know? Maybe whoever's doing this wants you to think Tomas is cheating on me. By not revealing the whole picture it throws suspicion my way."

"And why would someone want to throw suspicion your way?"

"Again, how the fuck would I know?" Roger stormed over to the window and saw multiple cop cars in the street. "What's going on?" He turned. "Why are there five cop cars on the street and two officers in our doorway?"

"Because, Mr Head was found in the underground car park of this building, Mr Dencott."

"What?" Roger and Tomas cried out.

Tomas struggled to his feet, and Roger rushed to his side to support him. "He was found here? Downstairs? When? How?"

Barden noted their surprise. "We got a call about a

suspicious looking scene in a car park and came for a look. We found the body of Mr Head lying between your two cars with three vials of coke."

"What do you mean he was lying between our cars?" Roger spat. "What the hell is going on?"

"It would seem Mr Head felt lovelorn and drove over here this morning, took an overdose, and died for the sake of love," Barden told him. "*Your* love."

Roger watched Barden's face and frowned. "What? What do you mean…?" His voice trailed off, and Tomas laid a hand on his chest. He covered it with his own as he looked at him. Tomas was confused and sick.

"It seems Mr Head was in love with you, Mr Dencott. He used his keys to scratch, '*Roger, I love you*', into your car."

"What!" exploded out of Roger. "*That bastard scratched my car?* Was *he* the bastard that did that a couple of months ago too? Was it him?" He wildly paced back and forth. "I'll kill him. *I swear to God I'll kill him.*"

"Did you, Mr Dencott?" Barden asked.

Roger stopped, hands on hips, staring at Barden. "What? Did I what?"

"Kill him?"

"Don't be absurd." Roger moved over to him. "*I didn't kill anyone, least of all Aiden Fucking Head.*"

Barden raised a brow. "Yet here he is, in *your* car park, next to *your* car, after scratching that he loved you into it. And yes, I found that report about your car, nasty business that was. Four tyres, sugar in the tank, needed a complete overhaul.

"Did he do that, too?" Roger asked. "Did he give it a second try?"

"Were you lovers, Mr Dencott?"

Roger blinked. "What?"

"Were you and Mr Head lovers?"

Another blink. "No. I told you we did one movie together years ago. We were never lovers. I never fuck my castmates outside of work."

"And yet, here you are with Mr Stephanopoulos." He glanced at Tomas. "Who doesn't look so good."

Roger moved to his side. "Sit down." He sat beside him. "You okay?"

Tomas shook his head. "I don't feel good."

"The pain's come back?" Roger rubbed his back.

"No. I just feel a bit light-headed." He covered Roger's hand with his. "I'll be okay."

"Plan on killing another lover, Mr Dencott?"

Roger's head turned sharply. "What? I didn't kill anyone and I sure as hell wouldn't kill Tomas. I love him."

"Of course you do, because you *never* fuck castmates out of work."

"Mmm," Roger mumbled. "It was different this time. We met and got together before Tomas started working for Marcus."

"Introduce him, did you?"

"No. I think that was Violet who'd found out about him through Bette Olander. Are we done?" He sighed and attended to Tomas.

"Afraid not, Mr Dencott. I must insist on you coming down to the station for a full questioning. We need to go all the way back to the beginning."

"What?" Roger protested. "You've *got* to be kidding me?"

"Are you refusing to come down to the station of your own volition?"

"Yes, I bloody well am," Roger said.

"Then, Mr Dencott, I am arresting you on suspicion of murder. You have the right to remain silent, anything you say or do will be used against you in a court of law. You have the right to an attorney. If you cannot afford an attorney, one will be appointed to you. Do you understand these rights as they have been read to you?"

"What? You can't be serious?" Roger clung to Tomas as the officers came over and produced cuffs. "You're arresting me for murder?"

"On *suspicion* of murder," Barden corrected and indicated for the two officers to take him.

They hauled him to his feet, put his hands behind his back, and cuffed him.

"I can't believe you're doing this, Barden. I'll have your guts for garters before the end of the day." Roger struggled as he was taken out of the room.

"Roger, Roger, don't do anything rash. I'll call Marcus. Roger, I love you," Tomas called weakly.

"I suggest you call an ambulance instead, Mr Stephanopoulos. You look ill." Barden frowned.

"I'll be all right, Detective, it's just a bug." Tomas's steely look of determination was all show, for he was a quivering mess on the inside. He waited for Barden to leave and close the door before collapsing on the sofa.

"Oh, God, oh, God. I feel, oh, God. Get a grip, Stephanopoulos. Your man's in trouble, and he needs you." Taking a deep breath, he phoned Marcus and told him what had happened. Marcus promised to get their lawyer down there immediately.

Next, he called Bette to cancel all sessions until further notice and told her what was happening. She promised to round up the troops if they were needed.

He grabbed his bag, made his way slowly downstairs, and caught a cab to the station, where stumbled inside to the front desk.

"You okay?" The clerk stared at Tomas.

"I don't feel good," he replied. "I'm here for Detective Barden. He brought a friend of mine in for questioning."

"Sure. I'll just give him a call." The officer made the call and directed Tomas to his office.

"You really need an ambulance, Mr Stephanopoulos," Barden said upon seeing him. "Do you do drugs, Mr Stephanopoulos?"

Tomas frowned. "No, I don't."

"Then what's making you sick?" Barden sat on the corner of his desk.

"I don't know." Tomas struggled to think. "Food poisoning…I don't know."

Barden frowned in concentration. "Lover boy's in with the lawyer. He was here within minutes of us bringing him in."

"Good," Tomas muttered. "Can I get some water?"

"Sure." Barden hit the cooler and was back in thirty seconds. "Here. So what have you been eating that would make you sick?"

Tomas sipped the cold water, feeling it slide down his parched throat. "I don't know. We had some Chinese the other night, we eat breakfast at home, I eat lunch at Bette's, and then we have something at the studio."

"Eat anything out of the ordinary?" Barden made notes in his book.

"No." Tomas shook his head. "I try to eat healthy food. Roger jokes about the food I do have. It's always the healthiest I can find. He hates my milk."

"He doesn't drink it?"

"No. Only I do." His eyes felt like sandpaper. "I want to see him."

"Not until he's finished with his lawyer, and then we talk to him. So it will be a while." He watched Tomas close his eyes, his hand drop the cup, and his head slump before he collapsed onto the floor. "Get an ambulance," he yelled into the station before tending to Tomas. "Wake up, damn it."

Ten minutes later the ambulance arrived and carted him away on a stretcher.

Barden burst into the interview room. "What poison have you been feeding Stephanopoulos?" He slammed his hands onto the table.

Roger and his lawyer jumped. "What?"

"What poison have you been giving the kid?" Barden repeated, leaning closer.

"I have to protest," the lawyer jumped in.

"I don't, I haven't," Roger cried.

"Bullshit," Barden yelled. "Stephanopoulos just collapsed in my office and he's been taken away by ambulance to the hospital. He's clearly not well, and I want to know what he's been fed."

"Nothing." Roger stood and slammed his hands on the table as well. He leant in close to Barden so they were nose to nose. "I haven't poisoned anyone, let alone my boyfriend. I love him; why would I want to hurt him?"

"What about the milk?" Barden went head to head. "You don't drink it?"

"No, because it's shit stuff and I'm allergic to it."

"Or is it because you poisoned it?"

"I'm done with this garbage," Roger said. "I want to go to him." He looked at his lawyer in a panic. "I want to go to him."

"Well, you can't," Barden sneered.

"Well, someone has to," Roger cried. "He can't be alone."

"So he won't die?" Barden asked.

"What? No! So he's not alone," Roger replied. "I want to go to him."

"No. You'll stay here until we're done and that kid is well enough to talk. Is there anyone else to call?"

Roger thought about it. "Call Bette Olander. She'll go," he told the lawyer.

"Fine," Barden snapped and shoved a finger at Roger. "*You* sit down. You're going nowhere." He raced back to his office and hailed the officers from before. "Get back to Dencott's place and get the carton of milk from the fridge. Get it to the hospital lab. I think there's poison in it and they can test Stephanopoulos. I think the poor kid's being put out of commission." The officers nodded and left.

Barden went back to his desk and laid out the paperwork. Dencott was getting rid of previous lovers so that Stephanopoulos didn't find out? Or so they didn't talk? But talk about what? What was Dencott hiding?

*****

Luiz had watched the proceedings from the street as Roger was taken away, and followed Tomas as he'd taken a cab to the police station, then followed the ambulance to the hospital. Putting his plan into motion, he'd gone back to his hotel and changed into the outfit he would need to blend in.

He parted his hair on the side and slicked it down before packing up his toiletries. Today, he was leaving, never to return. Today was the finale of his plan. All phases were accomplished, the end was nigh, and time was up.

Shoving his toiletry bag into his case, he picked up a picture of Tomas. He'd taken it in Mykonos when they were on the small island, away from prying eyes and Tomas was asleep in the afterglow of their lovemaking. His face was soft and serene as he slept, dreaming of things he'd done and was going to do. Dreaming of happiness such as he'd never known.

He kissed the photo. "God, I love you, Tomas. And now that Roger is gone we will be together, for always." He tucked the picture into his pocket and walked out to his car, depositing his case in the trunk. He returned to collect some blankets and a box of food, then shut the door and put them in the front seat of his car. Leaving the hotel, he drove to the hospital and parked near the closest entrance possible.

*****

Bette, Bertha and Willow made it to the hospital and stood guard outside Tomas's room. He was strung up with tubes and machines so there was no way anyone was going to get their Tomas, even if they had to fight off any attacker.

They watched as blood was drawn, and officers arrived, handing over a carton of milk which the doctor took away. They waited while Tomas was given drugs and the doctors came rushing back. They watched as the doctor ordered ten milligrams of some medication and then inserted it into the drug bag. And they listened while the doctor told them Tomas had been poisoned over a period of time.

They sighed in relief when they found out he was going to be okay. And when he was moved from the ICU to a private room they took a break.

Willow went off in search of food, and Bette went in search of a phone to call Roger's lawyer. Bertha went in search of the ladies' room and when she was done walked back to Tomas's room. As she turned the corner into the hallway, she saw an orderly pushing a patient into the lift at the other end of the hall. The patient *looked* like Tomas, and she stopped. *Why would…?* She looked up at the orderly, and while she didn't recognise the blond hair, she definitely recognised the aqua eyes.

"Oh, my God," she muttered as the doors closed. She hastened to Tomas's room to make sure it was him before pounding down the hallway in her jewelled orthotic slip-ons to the nurse's station, colliding with Bette and Willow. "He's gone," she shrieked. "Tomas Stephanopoulos has been taken. He's been kidnapped."

The whole hospital went into lockdown, and Bertha ran for the lift. "Come on," she yelled to Bette and Willow. "I know who took him."

"How do you know?" Bette asked on the way down.

"Because I know those eyes anywhere," she said.

They bolted out of the hospital and in the direction of the other entrance, seeing Tomas being loaded into the back seat of a car as they rounded a corner.

"Stop, thief, kidnapper," Bertha yelled, catching him by surprise.

He slammed the door and climbed into the driver's side before screeching out of the driveway and down the road.

"Oh, no, he's getting away," Bertha cried.

"But I got the licence plate and car make and model." Bette flashed the paper she'd written it down on. "Let's call Roger."

They hastened back to the public phone booth and called the station, asking to speak to Roger's lawyer.

Barden stayed with Roger while the lawyer took the call. He had a silent stare-off with him as they waited, hoping he'd say something. He didn't.

The lawyer came back in. "Stephanopoulos has just been kidnapped by a man dressed as an orderly. The women got the make, model, and plate of the car. The officers are checking it now, but they say they know who did it."

"What?" Roger stormed to his feet. "Someone kidnapped Tomas? Who? Who took him?"

The lawyer looked at him. "Some guy named Luiz Manning."

"Luiz?" Roger felt the wind blow out of him and slumped into his chair. "I thought he was out of Tomas's life."

Barden frowned. *Why does that name sound so familiar?* He quickly left the room and went back to his desk, poring through the papers until he finally found it on a list for ex-members of *Seralift*. Luiz Manning. Slapping the paper, he muttered "Knew I'd heard of you before." He barged back into the interview room. "*Who* is Luiz Manning to you?"

Roger looked up in a daze. "What?"

"*Who* is Luiz Manning to you?"

Roger shook his head in frustration. "No one. Not personally. I've never met him, but have heard all about him."

"So, why would he poison and kidnap Stephan-opoulos?"

Confusion set in. "What? Why would he poison…?" Roger vaguely asked.

"Well, unless *you* poisoned the milk lover boy drank, I'd say Manning did it to get you out of the way so he could take him. I had officers get the milk from your place and take it for analysis. Nerium Oleander. It makes you weak and sick, but only kills you after a large enough period of exposure. So who is he?"

Roger warily eyed the detective. "He was Bertha St John's fiancé for over a year. When they were in Mykonos over the summer he met Tomas, and they had a fling except Tomas didn't know he was Bertha's fiancé. They both dumped his sorry arse and came here. Luiz only turned up once at a club that I knew of until the other week when Tomas came across him at the beach. They had coffee in a café and talked." He shrugged. "That's it, as far as I know."

It was all starting to fit together for Barden. "Was Luiz the spurned lover?"

"I suppose," Roger said. "Look, what are you doing to find Tomas? He's sick, he needs care and needs to be in a hospital, not dragged off somewhere by some nut job."

Barden waved his hand. "Don't worry about it. We've got an APB out on the car. We'll find him. Would you put it past this Luiz to try and set you up for four murders so Tomas would be free for him?" He laid photos of all four dead porn stars before Roger on the table.

Roger thought about it. "I've never met the guy, but from what Tomas told me he was very controlling and obsessed on Mykonos. He followed Tomas to an island and kept him there overnight."

"Against his will?"

Roger blushed. "Well, no, that I know of."

"Mmm." Barden sat down. "So, what we have is a spurned lover who wants nothing more than his lover back and will stop at nothing to *get* him back."

*****

Luiz floored it out of the city and up the coast. He had to get the hell away from Miami and Florida so the cops couldn't get them. There was no way he was going down for all of the crimes he'd committed. Oh, no. Roger could take the rap for those while he sailed home free with Tomas.

He glanced over his shoulder. "Okay, Tomas? They gave you your meds, so you should be okay soon." He leant over and covered his lover with a blanket as he slept. "You rest, you need it." Knowing they had Roger in custody offered him some relief, and with luck, time to get as far away as possible.

He crossed the border into Georgia and debated which way to go. Across country would be good. He headed for Alabama and made it into a little town in Mississippi by nightfall. Crawling through the one horse town, he found a room in a seedy hotel, and under the blinking neon lights, carried Tomas into the room and closed the door.

*****

The man crawled to a stop outside the motel. He'd been tailing the car since Miami when he'd seen the man dressed as an orderly wheel Stephanopoulos out of the hospital and dump him in the back seat of his car. He'd taken off when recognised by three old broads and he'd followed since. He thought about how he could execute his plan and drove around the corner to find another way in.

*****

"Have you found him yet?" Roger stood up as Barden came into the room.

"Not yet. But Manning has to stop for sleep sometime," he said. "We'll find him. We've got officers checking every motel now."

Roger slumped into his seat with a sigh. "I should be out there looking."

"And where would you look?"

"I dunno."

"Well, then there's not much point you being out there because you'll only get in the way."

"But he needs me!" Roger yelled.

"What he *needs* is a hospital and real cops to find him," Barden replied. "Now, we have spoken to Ms St John, and there wasn't a whole lot she could tell me about Manning. She met him as a trainer, and it seems he trained her in the bedroom as well. They got engaged, and she broke it off when she found out he'd," he checked his notes, "seduced poor young Tomas with his sharp tongue and deft fingers. Not to mention his sizable cock that could do wonders." He grimaced and shut his notebook. "Gross. We've put out a description of him, but it's possible he's done a dye job on his hair and probably has Stephanopoulos covered over. We're doing everything we can."

*****

The man pulled to a stop at the back of the motel and turned off his lights. He had to be quick and quiet. No one could know. Pulling his gun from his pants, he rolled on the silencer and picked up his lock pick. He popped the trunk and left the car.

*****

Luiz was busy changing clothes and washing up. He needed to get Tomas out of the hospital gown and into something more appropriate. *Like me,* he thought, after taking off the gown and seeing Tomas naked on the bed. *Oh, God, how I've missed you.* He enveloped him whole, sucking the cock that had started it all. *Oh, God, how good it is.* He got a groan in return and swallowed when Tomas came.

He worked his way up his lean body and passionately kissed his mouth. Tomas responded weakly, and Luiz took advantage, rubbing their cocks together, sliding his hands all over. His leg was over Tomas as he explored the body he'd wanted for so long, and when he was done with the front, he rolled him over and started on the back. "Oh, God." He slid inside and tried to keep himself in check. "Oh, God, oh, God, oh, God," he squealed. Moving back and forth he was in pure heaven and heard not a single sound except for the beating of two hearts. He couldn't help himself, he sped up, thrusting wildly into the man he loved, so encapsulated he didn't notice the door open and close.

"Oh, God, oh, God, oh, God."

"Oh, God indeed," the man said.

Luiz's head spun around to see a man holding a gun and a bullet coming for his forehead.

Five down, none to go.

Luiz's blood splattered and he slumped backwards off the body of his lover, his eyes staring at the ceiling, his mouth in an o shape. O for orgasm? O for ecstasy? O for terror?

No one would miss Luiz Manning. Not his mother, Sheila Manning, who lived alone in New York with the exception of a couple of cats. She hated his guts and had disowned him at seventeen upon finding out he was a fag who fucked the underage neighbourhood boys, and so he'd run away to Miami and joined a studio making porn movies. And his sperm donor father, whom his mother had met in Santorini twenty-six years earlier and had a holiday fling with, certainly wouldn't miss him. No, Andros Poulos had never acknowledged his illegitimate son, or paid for him, and never would. For Andros Poulos *never* acknowledged his illegitimate children.

No, no one would miss Luiz Manning at all.

The man rolled Luiz all the way off and grabbed the clothes on the floor, slipping a hoodie over Tomas's head and pulling track pants up his legs. He noted the sizable package and moved on, tying sneakers onto his feet. He hefted Tomas over his shoulder and looked out the window before opening the door. Looking left and right, he silently closed it behind him and walked back to his car where he lifted the trunk and placed Tomas inside. All he needed now, was to get to Chicago.

*****

At ten-fifteen the next morning, the police rolled through town looking for a car. They found it in the *Shady Seeds Motel* parked out front of room 29. After knocking, they had the attendant open it and found the body of Luiz Manning dead on the bed. There was no sign of Tomas Stephanopoulos except for the hospital gown he'd been wearing. The officers radioed in and called their coroner.

*****

Barden heard the news fifteen minutes later, right after he heard the APB for a Carlo Stefan. Formerly Stephanopoulos. "What?" he'd muttered as he listened. Could they possibly be? He made calls to L.A. and found out that yes indeed, Carlo Stefan, formerly Carlos Stephanopoulos of Mykonos, was missing, feared kidnapped, and the police were on the hunt.

The man who had Carlos was headed east. Barden dug an old map out of his desk and spread it out. With a red marker he circled L.A., and moved east along the main highway, and then circled Miami and headed north. He left the lines unfinished, but circled a big space of the country. They could be going anywhere.

*****

The man pulled into a gas station. He'd driven all night and made it across Tennessee, but needed gas and food. Not to mention a hot shower and a pussy to fuck. He needed to lay his own cock in a good accommodating whore, and he couldn't wait. But first, he had to take care of this one little thing.

Standing at the counter paying for his food, he glanced out to see the man from the car behind looking strangely at his own. Walking outside, he found out why. Tomas was banging on the inside of the trunk, yelling out for help.

He didn't panic. He simply looked at the man, pulled his jacket aside to show his gun, and proceeded to get in his car while the man's pump flooded over. He drove away while the attendant came running out.

*****

An hour later, Barden got a call about a man being trapped inside of a trunk, yelling for help, and the owner of the car had a gun. The licence, TGS 333, had been checked and the plate stolen, but a description had been taken, and now there was an APB out for him. Barden uncapped his red marker and circled the town Luiz had been found in, the town the new guy had been found in, and connected the dots.

He was moving north.

He followed the main highway and came to a stop. He finished off the other line and found they could be heading in the same direction. He went to see Roger in his cell. "Does Stephanopoulos have a brother?"

Roger lazily sat up. "What?"

"Do I *really* need to repeat myself?"

"No." Roger sighed. "Two. Carlos and Pedro."

"Who also happen to be porn stars?"

Roger stood up, intrigued by where the conversation was going, and moved over to the bars. "What? Why? What's happened?"

"It seems that both brothers are in the porn industry and both have been kidnapped."

"What!" Roger exclaimed. "You're kidding."

"No. I've been in contact with L.A. Carlos has been missing for nearly twenty-four hours."

"Fuck," Roger said. "So, where are they going?"

"After detailing it all on a map, my gut tells me one place."

*****

The man pulled up behind an old dump site on the outskirts of some clunky little town in Kentucky. It was midnight, and he needed rest.

"Let me out, help," Tomas yelled pitifully, banging on the trunk.

"Ugh." The man got out, opened the trunk, and stuck his gun in Tomas's face. "Shut it, and you won't be dead."

Tomas lay back, shielding his eyes, dazed, confused and scared as hell. With everything that had happened, he had no idea what was going on, and he was sick, tired, and hungry. "Water," he croaked through dry lips.

The man slammed the trunk, dug through his supplies of food, and opened the trunk again. "Here." He handed over a sandwich and can of soda. "Now shut up." He slammed the trunk and settled back in the driver's seat.

Tomas greedily ate the sandwich and drank the soda. *Who the hell is he?* With a head that was pounding, he curled up on his side with his arm under his head. He didn't know what the hell was going on, but he wasn't about to find out in the trunk of a car.

*****

"Where?" Roger asked. "Where are they taking him?"

"Chicago," Barden said, proud of his detective skills and putting it all together. "Does he know anyone in Chicago?"

Roger thought about everything Tomas had ever told him and shook his head. "No."

Barden lost his wind. "Well, I'm flying out there to see what the cops know. You can stay here until I learn something." He left with Roger calling out behind him. After a quick rest at home and a four hour flight to Chicago, he was in the captain's office talking about the case.

"I think my guy's headed here, but I don't know why and I don't know where." Barden stood looking out at the grey clouds. It was ten o'clock in the morning.

"What could possibly be the point of bringing the kid here?" Captain Wallace asked. In all his forty years on the force, he'd never heard of such things, even though Chicago had been labelled a mob town. "And you say his brothers have been kidnapped as well?"

"Apparently." Barden turned around. "I got news of New York before I came here. But so far neither L.A.

or New York know where the kidnappers are headed."

"So, how did you figure it out?"

Barden smiled. "I just connected the dots."

*****

The man woke and checked his watch. Ten a.m. "Fuck." After taking a leak, he took off for the nearest gas station and kept an eye out for cop cars, but fifteen minutes later he was on his way with no trouble. He had Indiana and Illinois to get through, and the paper predicted rain.

The service attendant made a call. "I just seen that car you're afta, you know, the brown seedan…yep… yep…gas und food…he took off down the high heading north… Yep…yep…yep sir, thank you sir, yep sir, bye."

Feeling proud of himself that he had called in a wanted car and the potential reward it would pay, he didn't see the two fifteen-year-old kids sneak in the back door, or come up behind him. They raised their arms and blasted his brains out with their guns. He fell dead to the floor.

There would be no reward for Hector Veddler today. After all, no good deed goes unpunished.

The two kids raided the till, piled junk food into their bags, and took off the same way they'd come when a cop car pulled in. The cops were stopping to chat with Veddler to get a statement. But they were too late and called in a dead body instead.

*****

Barden kept in touch with his officers back in Miami. He also listened to the calls over the radio about the car being seen at a station, and then the call for the body of an attendant.

"Think he doubled back to get rid of a witness?" Wallace asked.

"Nah. I doubt he has the time." Barden marked off his map. "Oh, he's definitely headed here. Only two states to go."

*****

In the afternoon, the floodgates opened. He'd made it to Illinois and just needed to get to Chicago, where his boss was waiting to take care of the package. Considering some of the other jobs he'd taken on in the past, this one wasn't so bad. He only had to do away with one prick that got in his way, and the other was sleeping in the trunk.

He flicked on the radio and spun the dial around until he found an easy listening channel that played old songs he liked. Not the disco crap that was currently all the rage. He couldn't stand it and didn't know how anyone could. It all sounded the same and had no real meaning. The words were a bunch of mumbo jumbo and made no sense. He sang along to a *Carpenters'* song. Now this one had real heart. At least it had meaning.

The sky grew darker as he approached Chicago.

*****

It was dark when Barden looked out the window, even though it was only early evening. The storm covered the city and blocked out all light. He checked his watch. Seven. Where was he? He looked at his map and knew they couldn't be far.

An officer ran into the room and handed over a piece of paper.

"What is it?" Barden asked excitedly, leaning on Wallace's desk as he read it. "What does it say?"

"They've found Pedro Stephanopoulos and are headed to O'Hare."

"I knew it," Barden crowed. "Let's go."

They flew downstairs and into their cars, racing to the airport. The storm picked up and pelted them all the way until they made it under cover and spoke to someone in charge.

"Are there any planes leaving tonight?" Barden asked. "Private planes, I mean."

The manager called in the list and found there was one plane destined for Athens that had to leave tonight.

"That's it!" Barden exclaimed. "Stephanopoulos is Greek. If all three brothers are coming here that has to be a connection. Where's the plane?"

The manager checked. "Hangar 33."

After getting directions, they took off and saw a car scream past them in the same direction, pulling into a hangar. Barden, Wallace and ten officers followed in the shadows, raising their guns, and surrounded the car as the man got out. "Hold it right there, police."

The man, stunned that he had been found, put his

hands up. "What's going on? What have I done? Did I run a red light?"

"Open the trunk," Barden yelled. "Open it." He motioned for an officer to pop it and found Tomas Stephanopoulos dazedly looking up at him.

"Hello," came quietly out of Tomas's mouth as he peered up.

"Mr Stephanopoulos, welcome back." Barden and Wallace helped him out, but he fell to his knees. They propped him up on the trunk lip. "Still sick, I see."

"What is this? I did not know there was someone in my trunk," the man said, knowing there was only one way out. "What is going on? Have I been set up?"

"You know full well what's going on," Barden told him. "You killed Luiz Manning and took Mr Stephanopoulos. Why did you do that? For *whom* did you do that?"

"Luiz is dead?" Tomas mumbled, his brain foggy and his stomach sick.

The man eyed everyone around him and pulled his gun out of the back of his pants. Shots were fired, but before he could run far, a bullet from Barden's gun had flown into the back of his head. He hit the floor. Dead.

"Ah, geez." Barden stood over the body. "Another one snuffs it." He waved a hand at Tomas. "Let's get him out of here. Get some food into him."

After soup and sandwiches, Tomas was brought up to speed. He shook his head. "Luiz was behind all of this? Just to break up Roger and me to get me back? It seems too incredible to believe."

Barden spied trench-coated feds from across the airport. "Mmm, it does." He watched them keep on going and wondered why they were there.

"Barden." Wallace pulled him aside. "They're here. I just heard it over the radio; they're all here and headed for that jet."

"Let's go," Barden told the others before turning to Tomas. "*You* stay here and keep warm. We're going to find out what's going on."

"No." Tomas stood up. "If I was kidnapped by someone else for a reason, I want to see for myself and find out what's going on."

"It's safer if you're out of the way." Barden didn't have time to argue. "Besides, you're weak and sick, so stay here." He took off with Wallace and the officers.

"There's no way I'm staying here on my own." Tomas ran weakly from the room and followed them down the hall and out into the blinding rain. They made their way back to the hangar, but kept going. In the distance, they heard sirens, and on the other side of the hangar was a plane with the engine already running.

Running through the hangar, they skidded to a halt as the plane on the tarmac prepared for take-off.

"Is that it?" Barden yelled over the thunder. "Is that the plane we're after?" They watched the plane and saw trench-coated feds coming their way.

"Here's trouble," Wallace said.

Barden saw Tomas behind him. "You were supposed to stay inside," he yelled.

"Not on your life," Tomas yelled back and turned

to the right as sirens screeched to a stop in a hangar down the lane.

"Guess we're not the only ones after that plane and whoever the hell's on it," Barden said, watching as a man ran across in front of them following the plane. He was waving and yelling. "Who the hell is that?"

The trench-coated feds got closer. So did more sirens as they watched the man go down, and three cars scream past. They skidded to a halt past the dead body.

"What the blazes is going on here?" Wallace yelled.

The feds caught up to them. "What do you lot want? You shouldn't be here." He looked past them. "Who the hell are they?"

They all turned to see a small group of cops running for the cars on the tarmac.

"Don't know, but I guess we'd better join them." Barden took off with Tomas right behind.

Every single person in each of the three groups skidded to a stop in the pouring rain as the plane took off, and Tomas finally looked over at the group to their right and spied a familiar profile as that group looked at them. "Oh, my God...oh, my God..." He pushed his hoodie back for a better look and seconds later took off running for the man in the other group, grabbing him in a bear hug. "Pedro."

"Tomas. Oh, my God," Pedro cried, hugging him back. "Tomas!"

They didn't let go, staring as if they hadn't seen one another in years.

The cops all gathered round eyeing one another off, and the boys finally noticed they were being watched.

"Ah, this is my brother," they said at the same time.

"So, who's that then?" Barden asked, at the same time as a trench coat from the other group, and pointed to the first group of cops that had come tearing into the airport.

The boys turned to look in the pouring rain, arms still around each other, wiping the water from their eyes for a clearer look, to see a trench-coated man nod and point in their direction. The man beside him turned.

"Oh, my God," Tomas murmured, not believing who he was seeing. He knew that face anywhere.

About the Author

L.J. has been writing since 2006, when her first of many novels, *The Road To Vegas,* was born. In 2016 she created the *Porn Star Brothers* series about three sizzlingly hot Australian born Greek Island raised brothers who became the hottest porn stars in '70s America.

L.J. lives in Australia, loves '80s music, disaster movies, and collecting Jackie Collins books as Jackie is her inspiration and mentor.

L.J. Diva is the adult pen name for author Tiara King. You can find more about Tiara on her website; follow her on social media, or visit her publishing house, Royal Star Publishing.

Socials

tiaraking.com.au/ljdiva

royalstarpublishing.com.au

Sign up for _Tiara's_ Newsletter…

Make sure you're always in the know and never miss free exclusives, the latest news, book updates, and so much more with newsletters from…

tiaraking.com.au

Have you read these?

Or these?

NOVELS

Burning Desires
Anything for You
Falling for London
The Road to Vegas
Hollywood Dreams
The Billionaire's Dirty Little Secret

SHORT STORIES

The Body
The Perfect Plot
The Star of Your Own Crime Scene